FOREWORD

Morgan Adzei, a young Ghanaian writer, continues to show development in his second novel, "A Burning Desire"—a very educational and inspiring novel.

This second novel proved that he has deep insight and understanding about how Africans in the United States and Africa lived.

He is a much needed addition to the African writers of today and we hope he continues to show progress in this regard.

Professor John Henrik Clarke
Department of Black & Puerto Rican Studies
Hunter College of the City University of New York

INTRODUCTION

Like his previous work, *The Woes of the African Mother,* Chief Morgan Adzei's second book, *A Burning Desire,* should be carefully read by all Africans both at home (Africa) and abroad (the Diaspora).

Through the life of the young man Afolabi, born into a traditional village in Ghana who succeeds after many hardships in establishing a modern way of life in New York City, Chief Morgan Adzei examines the many problems that are central to the existence of all Africans today.

The negative socialization of contemporary Africans through contact with European exploiters and their exploitation of Africa's human and natural resources sets up in the youth "a burning desire" to experience negative Western ways (addictions, abortions, pornography, dependence on the modern conveniences of an industrial society, et cetera).

When the European-American value system of individual materialism begins to take its heavy toll, Afolabi and his friends come to realize that Africa has undergone a brain drain, and now lacks indigenous resourcefulness and creativity. As the United States' reactionary policies result in persecution of illegal aliens and welfare recipients alike, the Africans' "burning desire" becomes a new vision of a new Africa—without tribalism, false political boundaries or artificially created nations. A Mother Africa where all Africans can share in solving the challenges of drought prevention, the harnessing of her mighty rivers, the realizaton of a true African identity, "a burning desire" for Africa's redemption.

Dr. Leonard Jeffries, Jr.
Chairman, Dept. of African Studies
City College, New York City
February 21, 1984

ABOUT THE AUTHOR

Chief Morgan Adzei was born in 1948 in Ghana, West Africa. At the age of 15, he won two scholarships to attend either a Technical or Secondary School in Ghana. However, he refused both offers. Prodded by the District Commissioner of his region, he accepted one of the offers and attended secondary school. After graduating from secondary school, he gained national attention when his desperate letters reporting stories about the outbreak of an epidemic - CHOLERA in the village of Akplabanya was heard by the Ghana News Media.

Concerned by the suffering in the Continent of Africa, especially in his country - Ghana, he decided to write, to educate, to energize and to help in providing the basic needs that are lacking and making life very miserable for the people, the youths, the children and the mothers of Africa. He published his first novel - "The Woes of the African Mother" in 1982 and authored many more unpublished scripts. He has now set up a Scholarship Trust Fund for all the children born during the Great Exodus '83. He enjoys reading, writing, listening to soft and classical music, meditation and walking through parks and in nature. He adores the beauty of nature - trees, birds flying and singing, clouds moving across the sky, rolling hills and gentle mountains in a far off horizon.

ACKNOWLEDGEMENTS

The Author wishes to thank the following people for their help in the preparation and launching of this Book: Jerry Zimmerman and Bill Frumkin, my Publishers, through whose support and general expertise in the publishing field this work has become possible. James Gordon, Jr. for his wonderful editorial abilities. George Dzaba, President of Salvation Word Processing Services, Inc. and his hardworking Vice President, Patience Prebbie for the long hours spent in typesetting this book. Prof. Seth Ladzekpo and Attorney Alfred Ladzekpo (Togbe Asafokla), Henry & Pat Taffe', Johnnie Mae, Attorney Gweyne Wilcox and the Teachers at Workshop in Business Opportunities. Sister Kefa Nephthys and Brother Bill Jones, all the Family of The First World Alliance, Sons and Daughters of the Sun, Kwanzaa. Joy Dimone for her promotional abilities. David Lampel and WLIB Radio Station family for their great fundraising drive and information about the great exodus of 1983. Many thanks to Dr. John H. Clarke of Hunter College, Dr. George Simmons at Malcolm King College and Dr. Leonard Jeffries at New York City College, all of the Dept. of Black/African Studies; also, Author, Elizabeth-Harris, Kofi Dente, Julius & Emma Cobblah, John Aheto, Sonny Woanya, Anka Ra Semahj, Ernest N. Olaga, Emmanuel Anoe Lamptey, Richard Neequaye, Efeyinwa Acosta, Mohamed A. Dabre and Johnson Kuma who have made it a dream come true. Last but not the least, I wish to record my sincere love and thanks to my wife, Sophia Ardayfio-Adzei for her unflinching support and encouragement in this endeavor.

This Book is Dedicated to

My Parents
Azawovi Gbedemah
and
Alowosode Adzei
My Wife & Children
Sophia Ardayfio-Adzei
Yao (Jr) & Kudjo (Richard)
Brothers & Sisters
Ameyedowo, Yao,
Ablavi, Babie, Mansa
Ametorwonya and Lumorsi

And to

All who came to the rescue of exiled Africans
from one African soil to the other
in the past and present
The Seventh Day Adventist Church
Other Worldwide Churches
International Relief Agencies
Doctors, Nurses, men and women
of Africa and of African Descent
who have worked and are still working hard
to improve the conditions of their fellow Africans
at Home and Abroad

A BURNING DESIRE

CHIEF MORGAN ADZEI

<u>Ewe Proverb:</u>   Ne veviedodo hia la, miga wo fome o !!!

English   When perseverance is imperative, do not
<u>Translation</u>   hesitate !!!

A BURNING DESIRE

Chapter I

The crowing of roosters echoed throughout a little town near the River Volta in Ghana, signaling the beginning of a new day. "Cocorooco-oo, cocorooco-oo-cooo-oo, cocoroo co-oo, coo-ooo", they beckoned this day.

As the cocks continued to crow, a baby boy was delivered. With the beautiful sound of "Nei, neii, neiii," this brave little African announced his arrival into our tumultuous world. He was happy to be free at last from his mother's womb, perhaps he was the only person to have slept in that womb. A pregnacy that came a long way.

Sadly, his mother died of an unknown cause exactly four hours after his birth. With her dying breath she asked that the boy be named after his paternal grandfather, Afolabi. Thus the infant's family found itself mourning a passing instead of celebrating a birth. For them his sobs meant sorrow at the loss of a life they had known rather than joy at a new one. Tears rolled down their cheeks like the river that gently flowed through the town into the beckoning ocean many miles away. These were emotional displays for some of nature's bewilderments. Birth and death. His mother would have forever been very glad of his birth because she has always longed for a baby to care for.

On his seventh day of life the boy was "outdoored" according to ancient tradition. In this ceremony the child is taken out of the room for the first time, lifted to the sky, and told his name. The name he heard whispered in his ear was "Afolabi," as his mother had wished.

Afolabi found himself in the arms of his aunt and in those arms he would grow up and be treated just like her own son. As for his father, no one had heard from him for a long time.

Rebecca, Afolabi's aunt, was very beautiful. She looked like her late sister, but unfortunately she could bear no children of her own. She was very tall, with shoulder-length woolly hair. Her round, medium face sparkled with two big bluish eyes. Her countenance was dotted with a small mouth containing two evenly white sets of shining teeth covered by soft sensuous lips. When she smiled, she set envious enemies ablaze - and attracted loving people like a magnet.

She was truly a gentleman's lady, but her barrenness ultimately turned men away from her despite the attraction that the beauty of her inner and outer person would initially create.

Many African women had gotten children through the help of the dieties. Although Rebecca had traveled throughout the country, visiting many a shrine and praying that she might conceive, her efforts were in vain.

Her barrenness caused her much distress and posed a very severe societal problem for her. Not only was she insulted as a barren woman, but also she and her late sister had been labeled as witches. Their mother had long been called a practitioner of witchcraft and it had been rumored that she had taught it to them. Their mother was even accused of taking her womb from her stomach at an early age. It was superstition of the worst kind.

These rumors actually prevented Afolabi's father from marrying his mother. He did not even come to her funeral. Afolabi, then, had no father who cared for or even recognized him. His aunt never bothered to introduce Afolabi to him, although she knew his whereabouts.

Rebecca was persuaded to join a church in the town with Afolabi. After she joined this church, she found peace of mind and accepted everything that had transpired as the will of the Lord.

The rumors had alienated her and her son from the community they lived in and even from some relatives. As Afolabi grew up, he found himself faced with much hostility. The other children would not play with him although he could not understand why. So Afolabi and Rebecca had only each other.

Rebecca had a beautiful melodious voice and her singing gained her recognition in the church. She managed to learn the reading of the Bible with ease in the local tongue. Rebecca had accepted the Apostolic Faith and went to church regularly. She prayed to God to help her bear the ignorance of the society that continued to blame her for her barrenness and it seemed this prayer was answered.

Since the birth of Afolabi and his mother's tragic death, his father had never come to see him. So as Afolabi grew up, he knew nothing of his father or mother. Rebecca was very much annoyed with his

father's behavior and decided never to introduce
Afolabi to him. She never so much as mentioned his
name.

In the meantime, Afolabi's father had married many
women and fathered numerous children. This also
contributed to his indifference toward Afolabi.

Rebecca taught Afolabi the Christian faith. As he
grew up he became a very loving person, always going to
church with his aunt. Because of his obedient
attitude, she never refused any request of his.

Afolabi believed Rebecca was his real mother — he
knew nothing of her barrenness.

Rebecca, for her part, was careful to keep that
barrenness a secret. At times it greatly upset her,
but she found consolation in God. The peace of mind
that she and her son had both found in religion bound
them ever closer.

One Monday at noon, rain started to pour very
heavily, drenching the land much to everyone's
delight. It had been a long time since a single drop
had come down and everything had dried up. Now the
land, the lakes, the rivers, and the wells were all
filled with water once more. Quickly life had been
rejuvenated.

A gusty wind that came with the rain blew all night
Monday and all day Tuesday without stopping. It would
change directions from west to east, then east to
west. The clear blue sky was a beauty to behold as
thin motionless clouds formed rows across the vast
expanse of the bluish atmosphere. The temperature was
mild. Tuesday would have been a perfect day to work on

the farm but a taboo made Tuesday a day of rest. To disobey and farm on Tuesday was always dangerous. Farmers had no choice but to postpone all activities for the next day - Wednesday.

As Tuesday ,slowly developed into Wednesday with each passing hour, all was well and the whole village seemed to be smiling, the gong of the town crier was heard. More and more of the villagers' smiles faded with each ring.

"Fine evening to you all," the bellman said. Rebecca was very anxious to hear the news he brought, along with her nephew. She knew if it were death the people's ignorant superstition would cause them to be blamed. He began to speak but a shift in the wind made it difficult to hear the words. They strained to listen and the message indeed came through. Death had occurred.

"Well, I bring you sad news again. Chief Dunyo has died. There'll be a wake in his house tomorrow and burial will take place the following day."

"I knew it was death. I knew it," said Afolabi. "Oh, Chief Dunyo has passed away. All our elders are gone," Rebecca lamented.

"Is he related to us really? Afolabi asked. "Everybody in this town is related and it's unbelievable the way they fight among themselves."

"Yes, very close. That's grandmother's brother," she answered.

"Grandmother's brother--a very remote relation--not too-too-too-too close," he said in the spurious stammer he sometimes used.

Rebecca was surprised at his want of reaction to the old man's death. He watched with little concern as his aunt cried over the news. He did not even try to console her. They sat alone in their kitchen as the echoes of the gong reverberated spreading the news of the sad event to the people of the town. The oldman had died due to the sudden fall in temperature.

Afolabi's aunt was completely buried in her thoughts. Although she had lost her parents and sister long ago, the announcement had brought those past deaths to present memory. "Death, death, death. Yesterday death. Today death. What is going on, Lord? Why are we dropping like unripened fruits to the ground?" she lamented, as tears dripped down her cheeks.

The dead person had been a solid family man. He had circumcised the new-born Afolabi.

"But Mom, if people don't die, how can others have room to live? That's why it's important for people as well as other living things to die. After all, we kill chickens, goats, and fishes and eat them."

Afolabi's wise words surprised his aunt. She didn't believe a person his age could have so much wisdom.

Afolabi had begun schooling and was doing quite well. He had even been skipped a grade. He had won the admiration of all his teachers, but not that of his classmates who had been calling him "son of witches." They attributed his intelligence to his mother's presumed witchcraft, believing a ridiculous rumor that she had taken other people's brains and given them to him.

A BURNING DESIRE

Rebecca, by dint of hard work, saved money from her second-hand clothing store and put up a beautiful house in the town. She trained Afolabi very quickly how to love working as well. Because of this special relationship, he learned how to do things for himself, such as cooking and laundering clothes.

The hostility and resentment Afolabi met as he grew caused him great distress. He was shunned by his schoolmates and called the "son of witches," because he was always at the head of the class. His presence among his schoolmates scared them, but Rebecca's motherly love kept him calm and stable. This love withstood all the humiliations and resentments and Afolabi's studies did not suffer.

When he had finished grade school, Afolabi won a scholarship and enrolled in a secondary school in the town. It was a great moment for Rebecca to see her sister's son doing so well. She knew her sister's soul would greatly appreciate what she was doing. Rebecca was even proud and happy that her nephew had no friends other than his books.

Rebecca left Afolabi in charge of her second-hand store for the day while she went to Togbui (Chief) Dunyo's funeral. Early in the day, a girl he had seen in school came in to buy clothing. He had felt much attracted to her but had not dared to approach her because of his reputation. They had an amicable talk and fell in love immediately. She agreed to come by the house in the evening so they could go together to the movies, but when she arrived at his door Afolabi had already changed his mind. Since he knew that

Rebecca wouldn't return until after the burial, they didn't go out but stayed in the house instead.

Afolabi had long wanted a girl friend and now at last he had one. Beatrice, as she was called, was a very beautiful girl in her teens who looked almost like his aunt. This resemblance made Afolabi rush to get Rebecca's picture to show her. "Look at my mom. You look just like her."

"Your mom?"

"Yes, my mother."

"Are you sure?"

"You don't believe me? Or do you know my mother better than I do?"

"Just a joke," she said pleasingly.

Beatrice knew Afolabi's family history. She knew that Rebecca wasn't his mother. Although she was born in another town and had just moved into this one, she had heard every- thing about them. Nonetheless, she recognized the effect the disclosure would have on him and chose not to reveal anything.

Therefore, she agreed with him about the picture and they decided to put on some records.

The house, which had always been quiet and serene, was now noisy for the first time as Afolabi turned up the stereo full volume just for the two of them. They played old Cliff Richard and Jimmy Cliff numbers and enjoyed themselves and each other until the wee hours of the morning. It was as if a whole new world had opened up for both of them.

Rebecca spent a full week at the grandfather's funeral and Afolabi and Beatrice were together the

8

whole time. Sometimes, waking up to the sounds of the different traditional drummings at the oldman's funeral, they wished she could have stayed away even longer.

It happened that Afolabi was not in when Rebecca returned.

She noticed the picture on her wall was missing and turned and went into Afolabi's room. There was her picture with some earrings that she did not recognize. She now knew that Afolabi had brought a girl home in her absence. Far from being angry, she actually sighed with relief to know he had at last been able to make a friend. But she also decided to warn him against getting any one pregnant.

What troubled her more than anything else, however, was finding her picture in Afolabi's room, for it might mean that the secret of his birth had been revealed. Did he now know she was not his real mother? She seemed to be a little bit disturbed. Had she returned from a graveyard into a minefield or what? Many questions went through her mind.

If he had not learned the truth, she would warn him strongly against involvement with girls at his age. For now, education was more important than girls and must be his first priority. However, if he should find out the truth, she would tell him all about it. So, she waited patiently.

It was some hours before Afolabi returned. When he did, he made no mention of his dead mother. Now certain that he knew nothing of her, Rebecca then deciced to let him know she was aware of what had transpired in her absence.

9

A BURNING DESIRE

Afolabi was surprised his aunt knew. After all, Beatrice had always come to the house under cover of night leaving at dawn. With nobody recognizing the figure in the dark. Had someone told or was he at fault for being careless?

He said nothing and concentrated on cleaning his records. Anyway, he could think of no response and his silence confirmed his aunt's conclusions.

He was not happy the way this first romance was going. He wished no misunderstanding occurred between him and Rebecca. He valued the love she had given him for so long and hated the displeasure he was now causing her. Nonetheless, he did not feel he could give up his new love either. He would be more careful the next time. His first love experience was just too sweet to be let loose. He promised to be extremely careful.

Chapter II

Something dramatic was about to happen and this sleepy town would soon see changes in its social, economic, and political life.

The government of the land had decided to construct a bridge across the river that flowed through the town to facilitate the movement of goods and people to the neighboring countries.

As Afolabi spent his first year in secondary school, roads and living quarters were being built around the clock. For the first time, the town had a "night life." Engineers from other parts of Ghana, as well as from Germany, started to arrive in large numbers. Heavy equipment started to pour in, as billboards appeared to proclaim the new joint-venture.

Just as the German engineers were settling in, a revolution that toppled the ruling government quickly replaced the Eastern Block nationals who were teaching in the secondary school with American and Canadian teachers.

Work began in earnest on the project, providing job opportunities to the youths as well as other able-bodied persons in the town. Many job-seekers from within and without the country were given jobs. Social and economic life improved, as people who had never earned money before began to make handsome cash bi-weekly. For the first time, there were day and night shifts for the workers.

The town's youths immediately began copying the ways of the foreign workers. They started wearing psychedelic pants and cowboy hats,as well as drinking beer and chain-smoking, now that they had money to buy cigarettes.

Prostitution and stealing, dubbed western evils, became common. While others began to worry about these social evils, Rebecca and Afolabi enjoyed peace of mind. Nature had given their enemies something to worry about. Now more young girls were becoming pregnant and many gave birth to mixed-race children.

Some folks did not want to accept the changes brought by modernization and tried to oppose them, but the forces of change were overwhelming. They could not do anything but accept the changes as a fact of life, at least for now. It was not by their will that a river flowed through the town. It would not be by their will that a trade route would pass through it either.

The next year began with disappointments for Afolabi. Beatrice, his girl friend, failed to qualify for enrollment in the school. Both had wanted to be enrolled in the same boarding school so that they could be close to one another.

Afolabi was even more depressed by her failure than she was. Instead of bringing his emotions under control, facing reality, and realizing the importance of his education, he decided he would not return to school.

Afolabi was destined to be a leader, but he was not developing the judgment he would need, for want of a father's direction. Rebecca, nonetheless, did the best she could with him, urging him to go back to school.

A BURNING DESIRE

"You'll have no difficulty finding another lover if only you return to school and study very hard and become a scholar," she said. "Only then will girls float around you like bees."

Beatrice, for her part, did not like Rebecca's constant interference in their love affair; she started to drift away slowly to another man, although Afolabi was not aware of it at the time.

On her job she fell in love with a German engineer, nicknamed "Mr. Red" from the deep sun tan he had acquired while on duty. She had to decide between two lovers, one white, the other black. Beatrice thought about the fact that Afolabi's family was considered "tainted." He was also a student with no job and was not yet in a position to keep any promise he might make to her. The German had money and a job and had also promised to send her overseas. Whether or not he intended to keep his promise, Beatrice did not know.

"Mr. Red" had something of a reputation in town for having fathered many children there already. Why hadn't he sent them overseas? This question troubled Beatrice.

In the meantime, she conceived by Afolabi, but found she was able to convince "Mr. Red" to send her overseas by making him think it was his. He even handled all the documents for her. Beatrice was very fortunate. She became the first woman to go to America in this town. Breaking the myth about going overseas.

Her sudden departure overseas surprised Afolabi, as well as her own parents, and dumbfounded almost everybody. Afolabi promised himself he would find her again, wherever she had gone.

13

A BURNING DESIRE

Chapter III

Beatrice's departure brought a new awareness, a new dawning in the history of this developing town and left a controversy behind to the detriment of her parents.

Beatrice had told her parents that she was carrying Afolabi's child. She did not, however, wait long enough to clarify the situation. Since her parents knew she had been going with Afolabi and "Mr. Red" at the same time, they did not understand how the pregnancy related to her rapid departure. But she had left and she had said Afolabi was the father of the baby. Her parents, then, had no choice but to accept her words and deal with the presumed offender.

In this community, if a girl was in school and became pregnant, the parents would demand damages in the Chief's Court in monetary form, calculated from the time she started school up to completion of the last form. The parents of the man would have to pay, or if the man himself had the means, then he would have to pay. This law had been instituted to discourage teenagers from getting pregnant while still in school.

Afolabi was now implicated. Although the chief plaintiff was abroad, the father wanted to be compensated. Rebecca argued convincingly on her nephew's behalf, asserting that "Mr. Red" rather than Afolabi was the father of Beatrice's baby. But who would dare to bring a white man to the Chief's Court and make him pay? As a result of rebecca's defense, the case was thrown out.

After winning the case, Rebecca became more involved

in trying to persuade her nephew to go back to school.
"You will lose for good if you don't go back. The girl
you claim to be so madly in love with has gone abroad.
She will come back as a 'V.I.P.' If you're that stupid,
don't go back to school and one day you'll be her
carwasher. You'll be losing twice over. I've suffered
from not having an education. That education could
have brought me to America. I wouldn't have had to
sell my precious body to foreign workers to get there,'
she added much to Afolabi's annoyance. "Anything you
want in life I promise to help you get it."

Finally, Afolabi was persuaded to return to school.
Just three weeks after returning to the campus, he
nearly met his death. At midnight, when the campus was
quiet, some men came to kidnap him. They managed to
detach his bed from the lower portion and took him away
from the dormitory as he slept.

As they stepped out of the dormitory and were
heading towards the bushes, a strong whirlwind suddenly
began blowing. A lady emerged from nowhere dressed in
a white flowing gown and knocked the two men to the
ground. She touched Afolabi gently on the forehead,
waking him up. He was being carried away dead asleep.

"This is your mother's ghost. I'm watching for
you. Don't worry."

He heard those spoken words but thought he was
dreaming.

When Afolabi realized where he was, he began to
yell, beating his palm against his mouth to produce a
loud noise that awakened the student body. By this
time, the two men had gained consciousness and taken to

their heels. Luckily, Afolabi was unhurt.

While home on semester break, Afolabi found out that the two men had been sent by Beatrice's parents to kill him. Only his mother's apparition had saved him.

He now knew that Rebecca was not his mother. He surmised that some of the townspeople must know what her relation to him really was. But whom would he dare to ask? Of course, his father must know, but his father was a total stranger to him. Afolabi remembered Beatrice questioned him faithfully about this relationship. But she too had left the country.

At all events, he reasoned, she had always been to him as a mother. They could not be any closer had she given him birth, for she was all he had. He decided, then, to keep the knowledge silent that the apparition that had saved his life was really his mother and not the woman who now cared for him so lovingly. He would continue to speak of her as his mother and think of her as all that a mother ever could be.

Chapter IV

Construction had now ended and most of the foreign workers had gone, leaving behind their monument to Western ingenuity--the bridge. It was magnificently built, spanning the widest part of the river. It had taken them a year and nine months to complete, but when they left, the town's new-found prosperity left right along with them.

The German engineers who had fathered children in the town had left an indelible mark on the face of this once sleepy little ferry port.

The stores that had flourished at the peak of the construction lost sales, closed down, and moved out of town.

It had become very obvious that the bridge wouldn't do any permanent good to the inhabitants of this town. Drivers no longer stopped in the town to buy the things they needed. Soon the once-jubilant busy town began to be too quiet.

Rebecca had enjoyed those beautiful busy months of economic activity as many workers bought from her second hand clothing store. Like any business person in slack season, she began to get depressed. The general active population of the town was the young people who had drifted away as soon as work ended, refusing to go back to the traditional farming. Her goods were no longer moving, so she sold out everything before the boom town became once again a quiet village. She had little with which to support herself and Afolabi, so she started to go fishing for oysters in the river where they were indeed abundant.

One day she went fishing by herself as usual and a huge crocodile basking on the sand, unseen by her, grabbed her, dragged her to the bottom of the river and killed her. Since she had not informed anyone she was going fishing, no one knew of her death.

It was only the next morning when some girls who had gone to draw water saw her pan floating on the river. A floating pan usually meant an oyster fisher had perished. They ran and informed some fishermen living nearby who retrieved the pan and concluded the worst.

Announcement was made by the town crier of a lost fisherwoman. Still no one could identify the lost person.

Word reached the school. Afolabi, knowing that Rebecca had gone fishing alone, asked permission to be released so he could go home and check on her. He found the house deserted. He then ran to the police station and identified the pan. It belonged to Rebecca.

The search for the body had until now proved futile. It was imperative that the body be found and removed from the water, because the river was the main source of drinking water for the villagers. If the body remained there, it would soon be polluted.

Some elders were called to look for the dead body. What they were to do was regarded as unchristian so the church leaders rejected it. But if the dead body was not retrieved, then everyone's life was in danger. There weren't any Christian methods for retrieving the drowned, so they gave up.

It was about noon when the chief priest came to the the river. Libations were poured and the gods were asked to show where the body was. A young boy was handed a calabash full of the river water. After some incantations were said, a small body appeared in a corner of the calabash, at a confluence where a small river entered the big river; it wasn't far from where Rebecca had gone fishing.

Now that they knew where the body was, they had to retrieve it.

Afolabi gave his full attention to the unfolding African ritual. He had been kept away from such things by the very person whose body was being sought. He prayed inwardly that whatever body they turned up would not be hers.

As the ritual was performed, the divers downed a glass of a local distilled gin and jumped into the water near the spot located by the chief priest.

For some reason, they returned empty-handed and chatted with the chief priest before going down again.

In a flash, Rebecca's frigid body was brought up, missing an arm and a leg. When Afolabi saw it, he was overcome with emotion and burst into tears. Soon he collapsed and was rushed to a clinic in town. He wept and went for days without eating and was still sick when Rebecca was buried.

Rebecca had been the only person he could lean on. She was everything to him and life seemed vain without her. His mourning lasted many months. Now that she was gone, he was completely alone. Beatrice, his first and only girl friend, had left the country long ago.

19

He hadn't stopped longing for her even before losing his aunt; he had never before felt so depressed and hopeless.

Afolabi had stopped going to school or church and soon found himself unable to control his mind. He was bored, as the town had gone dead once the bridge was finished and even the unhealthy excitements that the town's brief experiment with prosperity had brought in its wake such as prostitution and gang fights were no longer in evidence.

To fight his boredom and loneliness, Afolabi started smoking marijuana and drinking. Since there were no more jobs in town and he had no income to support his bad habits, he began to sell some of his aunt's property.

The church tried to draw him into its fold, but he was not interested. He had given up on the Christianity that had helped both him and his aunt withstand the town's hostility. And to think the church had once had this pariah in mind for a pastor!

Afolabi started losing confidence in himself and having recurrent nightmares about his personal survival. The kindnap attempt had made him feel vulnerable. He wanted to go overseas to learn about America and to see his girl friend and unborn baby; he would marry her and bring them home with the knowledge of the things that made America or Germany so great and powerful. Of course, he had heard and read about them. He had also seen how good a job they did on the bridge. Perhaps Beatrice's relationship with the german engineer had really been beneficial after all. If only he could go and meet her and if both could work hard to import the knowledge gained overseas to change their own ignorant society!

Afolabi knew it was ignorance and superstition that had made it possible for his aunt to die and for his father to ignore both him and her. These same twin evils were responsible for his girl friend's painful break from him and the attempted kidnaping.

Had not superstition and ignorant gossip likewise deprived his aunt of the love of friends and relatives, leaving her alone in the world? Had she not had to go fishing alone, she might not have died.

Afolabi gave up and was going to leave. He was packing when some church members called at the door. When he heard them, he was very annoyed, for he thought they had come to offer consolation and invite him back into the fold. But he had already made up his mind he wanted to go abroad.

"Would you mind coming back later?" he called to the knock.

"We just want to deliver a short message to you from the pastor," a voice answered from outside.

"Okay, come on in."

They explained that the night before, the pastor had revealed to them a message he had received from God. The message was: "Take possession of Rebecca's house immediately."

This was an obvious ploy on the part of the pastor to get the beautiful house Rebecca had built. It was better than any in town. She had saved money from her hard work as a trader and farmer and put up a magnificent house--something not easy for a woman with no husband.

The visitors continued, "Afolabi, God wants this house for the church."

"What? Who did God say this to?"

"Pastor," was the confident reply.

Afolabi reached for a wrapping of marijuana and lit it. He dragged on the "joint" and exhaled through his nose. He offered some to the visitors but they declined. His head started spinning with questions and answers.

Afolabi sat down and thought about this strange news. He felt guilty about the bad habits he had acquired and about having had to sell some of his dear aunt's property to support them. He knew Rebecca had been a pillar of the church and was afraid her ghost might return to haunt him if he refused. Therefore, he did not argue. He gave them Rebecca's duplicate keys.

They thanked him, somewhat surprised at his ready cooperation. As they were leaving, he told them to return in the evening to lock the doors, since he intended to travel that very day.

Afolabi's lack of security and confidence and his unfounded fears had cost him a house he rightly owned!

However, this spurious arrangement would benefit him not in the too distant future.

Chapter V

Afolabi arrived in Accra with great expectations. Life was certainly better here than in his home town. He blamed himself for not having left sooner. He had come only after wasting much time, energy and most of all his money trying to fight boredom there.

He had enough money left to last him for a few months, provided he was thrifty. But life here would not encourage thrift. Girls and movies abounded, as did drinking and dancing bars. Everything that could make one forget thrift and choose to be extravagant was much in evidence and quite inviting.

He soon found many people in the city who had avoided him in his home town. Some were graduates, others school drop-outs. All seemed to have the same goal: to leave the country and "become somebody." Where would they like to go? Some were feverishly preparing to go to Europe or America, some to Nigeria. No one wanted to finish school and "return to the field." Those with degrees or mere certificates wanted nothing to do with traditional method of making a living, such as carpentry, masonry, or blacksmithing. They had come from the countryside to the city clutching huge briefcases manufactured for real businessmen. And they always introduced themselves as businessmen (the business office as well as the business itself compactly packed into the briefcase.) Following footsteps of predecessors who manufactured nothing, produced nothing consumed a lot of foreign items but proudly called themselves businessmen. With degrees in Business

23

Administration but no business to administer. What a shame! what a sheer ignorance!.

Afolabi was very happy the hostilities he had to endure in his childhood were at an end. He found friends who wanted the same things he did.

Although most of them had no one in the United States, they were very eager to go. Afolabi was luckier than any of them. His friend, Beatrice, had left long ago with his unborn bady. By now she must have given birth.

Since he had a little family there, Afolabi considered himself closer to America than any of his friends. However, he did not know how to get there. He had neither passport nor visa.

At this point, Afolabi was befriended by a man named Joe Galas. Joe had a passport stamped with a visa but no money to buy an airplane ticket. He helped Afolabi get a passport very quickly. Afolabi, in turn, promised to help him with the ticket.

One day Joe inquired, "I heard you mention something about your deceased monther's house being given to a church."

"Yes," Afolabi answered laconically.

"Did she leave it to the church in her will or did you decide to donate it to the pastor so he would pray for a passport and visa for you?" He burst into laughter at his own words.

"I was in the house preparing to leave when two members of church came with a message that the pastor said God spoke to him to get my mother's house for the church," Afolabi explained.

24

"Why did you agree to that ploy?" Joe fired at him. "Look, a preacher did the same thing to a friend of mine whose father happened to be a member of the church and owned a lot of cocoa farms. As soon as the old man died, the church took possession of the farms, claiming God had told them to do it."

"I guess I got taken in by a man who used the name of God falsely," Afolabi said, feeling very small and stupid.

"That's exactly what happened," Joe went on. "Why didn't you tell anyone in your family? Is your father also dead? Have you no uncles, aunts, brothers or sisters to fight for you?" No knowledgeable person in your clan?" No B--r-a-i-n?

Those questions made Afolabi realize how alone he was in the world and he could not hold back the tears. Joe began to walk to and fro. Going nowhere but hoping for answers.

Joe would not comfort him with sympathy, that eternal weakener of resolve. Instead, Joe shored him up with encouragement, as would a wise friend. "You need a plan of action," he said. "And I'm going to give you one. You've first got to expose that phony preacher and get your house back. Second you've got to find your relatives, wherever they are, especially your father." Is that man alive? Or he'd left the world of time to the world of timelessness?

A false religious fear made Afolabi still reluctant to try to get the house back. He wanted to forget about it. But Joe wouldn't let him. "Did you sign any legal documents relinquishing your rights to the house?"

25

"No."

"Then the house is still yours."

"Are you sure?"

"If you're not certain, then let me go take it for myself," Joe answered laughing. "I'll take the church too while I'm at it and throw out the preacher. I'll bet I can preach better sermons than he does anyway. He's probably doing all sorts of underhanded stuff the members don't even know about."

Joe's motives were not entirely altruistic. His visa was to expire in four weeks and he was counting on Afolabi to give him some of the money from the sale of the house (if it was to be sold) to help him get to the U.S. Joe had been able to get his visa renewed a number of times, but this last time the consul had warned they would not give him another extension.

"I can take you to your home town and help you get the house back. I can get it back for you in seconds," he urged.

"That's very nice of you, Joe, but I'd prefer to leave everything to God," said Afolabi.

His attitude shocked Joe greatly. He thought of him as weak and foolish, lacking in aggressiveness and dynamism. Curiosity about how the traits had developed prompted Joe to enquire about his father.

"Where is your father?"

"Why do you want to know? asked Afolabi.

"Oh, just to see if he can come to our aid," said Joe, concealing the real intent of the question.

Joe Galas had finished college with a B.S. in biological science and was far ahead of Afolabi in

26

knowledge. He didn't like the salary offered him so he was trying to leave the country.

"Hey, Afolabi, I want to really help you and possibly myself in the long run. Let's do something about that house. Even if you leave everything to God to settle, hoping He'll demolish the house or set that church on fire in ten years or a thousand years, that will never happen. Again, if I were you, wanted to go overseas, and had property I could sell for my passage and expenses, I wouldn't hesitate a day to do just that. Look, now you seem to be content with the few dollars you have in the bank. In one year, that money will be gone. Then you'll find out the difference between being up the creek without a paddle and crossing the Atlantic in a luxury liner," he said laughing.

"Joe, right now my problem is to locate my father."
"I asked you before where he was, but you didn't answer me," Joe reminded him.

Afolabi fell silent.

"Is he in your home town or living somewhere?"

Afolabi still did not answer so Joe decided to drop the subject.

"Well, Afolabi, since you seem to be more concerned with going to America, let's solve that problem first. You may indeed locate your father, but he might not be any help to us in terms of finance."

Truth to tell, Afolabi's mind was still on the question he had refused to discuss with Joe: his father. He was really worried about the fact that for so long he had never made any attempt to trace his

27

father's whereabouts, something he should have done when Rebecca was alive. Instinctively, he knew finding his father would solve many problems for him.

That Joe might trouble him no further, Afolabi decided to buy him the ticket. As for the house, he refused to try to get it back from the pastor. He was afraid the consequences might be fatal to him.

Joe was very happy that he finally got the plane fare to depart. A small party was organized for him. Many girls dressed in tight Jeans came to his party. Joe introduced Afolabi to some of the females at the party.

"This is the next person in flight to USA - Land of Believers", said Joe. Opening up the foors for contact among aspirants.

Afolabi immediately became attracted to one of the girls (Adzoa by name) who also wanted to go to America and they became friends. He promised to take her along to America as soon as his papers went through. Words girls wanted to hear even though they contain neither vestige of truth nor hope.

Adzoa's love for Afolabi and her desire to go overseas made her submit to him thoughtlessly even though he was not as well educated as she.

A BURNING DESIRE

Chapter VI

Three months after Joe had left for America, Afolabi had made Adzoa pregnant. Fearful of the consequences from his past experience with Beatrice, Afolabi quickly sought advice from a pharmacist.

The pharmacist gave him some pills that he claimed would induce an abortion. Afolabi gave Adzoa the pills although he knew nothing of the product or its safety. Adzoa, who was a first-year college student, was very eager to abort the pregnancy, for examinations were near and she did not want to fail. She wanted to finish her studies and further her education overseas.

Adzoa believed the pills Afolabi gave her were safe and took them as directed, informing no one in the house of her situation. Within two days, she started bleeding profusely from the mouth and nostrils. She was rushed to the hospital where she died moments after.

None of Adzoa's relatives knew anything about Afolabi. After her death, the rest of the fatal pills were found under her pillow, but no one could make out the trademark or had any idea how to locate the pharmacist. An autopsy revealed Adzoa's pregnancy and it was then inferred that she had taken the pills to induce an abortion.

At her funeral the headmaster warned all the young people present about abortions.

"There is a strong wind blowing -- an abortion wind -- that is destroying fruits in the bud and the very trees that are to produce them, our life-trees, are in danger," he said.

A BURNING DESIRE

"We must all build within us strong fortifications to stop its penetration. Let the young girls bring their boy friends home and introduce them to their parents. This will stop unnecessary abortions, since most of the abortions we are seeing stem from fear of parents and parenthood. Most important of all, young boys and girls must learn to take preventive measures. If you know how to open the door, you must know how to close it.

"I want to sound a special warning to our young mothers and mothers-to-be: don't give in too quickly to those who come from America, Canada and Europe wearing platform shoes, beautiful shirts and perfumes and making gifts of these things to you. They ride around in posh cars and promise to send for you as soon as they return. But all these promises are nothing but empty talk. Whether they came from USA or Europe, they are suffering over there. Life isn't gorgeous there. They're liers." Instead of saving hard earned cash to open up jobs for their brothers and sisters, they come to blow it and return to face harsh life of working for others.

"You don't cross a river when that river is flooded. You cross a river when that river is at low tide. Marriage works better when both couples work together to flood their homes with spiritual as well as material goods. You marry when that loving body is at low tide, and by your sweat, toil, and wit that low-tide body shall be flooded with loving happiness through generations unto generations.

"Our sister is gone but I hope today's message will

help to prevent more such tragedies. May she rest in peace."

This second incident left Afolabi very disturbed. He left Accra very quickly for his village. He was confused. Pain and fear went through his heart as he became very uncertain.

On the way home, he decided to try and find his father, whom he assumed to be alive somewhere. Perhaps finding him would make his life more meaningful. The only person who might be of help to him was the pastor, so he was glad he had not listened to Joe Galas after all. He was very sure that had he gone to demand the house, the pastor would definitely not cooperate with him in providing information about his father, which was the most important preoccupation of his thought at the moment.

It had been a year since he left town and when he returned to his aunt's house, he saw a complete change. The pastor had moved into the house and planted flowers around it. It was very beautifully maintained. Perhaps God had actually spoken to the pastor to take over the house. He knew that had he been around the house might possibly be defaced. If not sold cheaply to someone to support his drug habit.

He was warmly welcomed into the house by the minister. He had grown up in this house and was glad to be back. After leading an unhappy life in the city where all his money had evaporated into thin air, he looked very hungry and the preacher ordered that he be served some food. At least, by having someone in the deserted house to talk to he could as well put aside his problems.

31

A BURNING DESIRE

While Afolabi enjoyed his meal, the man of God tried to figure out the reason for his visit. The answer was not long in coming.

"Pastor, I need some answers about my background."

"Sure, I don't mind. Go ahead and ask anything you want to know," he assured him.

"You know about Rebecca whose house this is," he said. "I also want to know about my father. Rebecca didn't tell me anything about him before she died. Of course, I was foolish not to ask her anything all the years she was alive," he said as he started to cry.

"Don't cry. Blessings abound in all things created by God."
The preacher wiped away his tears and immediately answered his questions.

"Well, first of all, I'll tell you that you're now a man. Based upon that assumption, I hope you'll take everything courageously," he advised him. "You know Rebecca was not your mother."

Afolabi was silent at this revelation for he had already learned it from his mother's apparition.

Your own mother died when you were about four hours old," the preacher continued. "Rebecca was your aunt, your mother's sister. She took you and raised you, in keeping with African tradition. You should be very proud of that tradition."

"I'm enjoying the story. It's just like a movie I saw in the city some months ago," Afolabi commented at this point.

"let me hear it," the preacher replied.

"Yes. There was this fellow whose father abandoned

32

his mother as soon as he was born. It was during the depression and no money was coming in. He went crazy and moved to a deserted village in a desert near Mexico. Here he built a beautiful palace from rocks and bequeathed it to his son. I was thinking from my story that perhaps my father might build a fortune for me too somewhere."

"That's a beautiful story and a beautiful idea. Who knows? Your father might do the same for you, if not in the form of a palace, then in some other kind of wealth.

"Can you tell me where he is? Afolabi finally asked. "Many years ago I heard he was herding cattle in a town about fifty miles from us," the pastor answered.

"But cattle rearers always move from one area to another in search of fertile green pastures for their herds. Try there anyway. If you don't find him there, you might at least be able to trace him from there.

"That's exactly what I'll be doing," Afolabi said. "But you know something, my aunt was a beautiful kind person. I always thought she was my real mother until the night of the apparition." He then told the pastor the story of the maternal ghost who had saved him from being a kidnap-murder victim.

The pastor commented, "You know we Africans believe in the continued presence among us of our loved ones who have died. Because of that, even though they are invisible to us, we believe we're visible to them and that they are guiding, directing and protecting us from misfortunes.

"This conviction also makes us take care of our orphans and it's very rare to see them mistreated. You see, in our way of thinking, you're as much a son to your aunt as you are to your mother, as you saw. That's our traditon."

"I'll never forget my aunt and all our traditions."

"See that you don't," the minister concluded.

The next morning Afolabi set out to find his father. Before he left, the pastor prayed for his success.

A BURNING DESIRE

Chapter VI

All the information given Afolabi by the minister was very accurate and he was able to locate his father without difficulty. Afolabi's father, Kwame by name, had indeed been rearing cows. He was well-known and respected in the town. He was also very ill.

Kwame had married many women and fathered a lot of children. Many of them had grown up and left town. In fact, only the youngest and smallest remained in the house with him, along with his four wives. Altogether, the outside household numbered 20 people.

The two greedy wives wanted him to die so they could share his property and a senior wife was spearheading a plan to hasten his death.

Afolabi had been amazed at his father's affluence when he first arrived at the farming village. Kwame had two big ranches all full of cows of different sizes and shapes.

Because of this wealth, many false fetish priets had been offering their services to him at exorbitant prices. One had just arrived to attend to his healing after many had failed and from the onset he demanded a dozen cows and a huge sum of money. All this had to be paid before he even consulted the gods.

Afolabi sensed that deceit was at work everywhere in this household, but felt there was little he could do, for he remained an outsider in his father's house. Only, as the most enlightened member of it, he knew his father would recover if taken to a hospital, but the voices around him said the contrary.

The third day after Afolabi arrived in his father's village, the old man's condition seemed to be deteriorating very fast. The priest's healing powers were as false as a desert mirage. Instead of providing relief for this sick old man, he was simply relieving the boredom of village life by drumming incessantly and entertaining the able-bodied household rather than helping the dying Kwame.

On the fourth night, as Afolabi slept, he received a long visit from his mother's ghost which would help not only his father and his ignorant wives and children, but himself as well.

"Afolabi, I'm your true mother. I'm going to tell you a lot of things and they must be carried out.

Afolabi began snoring very heavily.

"When you get up this morning, immediately go to your father, introduce yourself to him as his son.

"I know how disappointed you were when you finally traced him and found him, but couldn't communicate with him or even enjoy his embrace. Your worries seemed to increase as you saw wealth around you but couldn't enjoy any of it. Your father himself is not enjoying his wealth. Neither are his children. Instead of using the wealth to better himself and his children, he worships it, leaving his children--your brothers and sisters--illiterate and ignorant. After his death his wives and children would enjoy the wealth. Something they actually planned to happen to him. "Don't let any of his wives give you food. After they learn you're his long-lost son, they'll try to kill you by poisoning your food. They may be thinking that you'll be taking

36

over when he dies. But also accept nothing in the form of gifts from your father. Anything he could give you would be worthless. The only thing you need is his recognition.

"Help him get well. You know your brothers and sisters as well as his own wives are just interested in seeing him die. They have no love for him. The real illness that he and the others are suffering from is ignorance.

"You'll have an opportunity to leave this country for a place whose name is music in the ears of many jobless youths here in this country who would like to go to see it for themselves. You'll love it. You already desire to go there. Help is forthcoming. But don't take anything from your father's domain. What you'll be getting in this beautiful land will be more than what he would be able to give you anyway. You should only be happy that you've found the man who brought you into this world. You'll not go there to enjoy but to learn the things they do to make life happy and return to do the same for your ignorant relatives. "I'll be detailing to you the things you'll be encountering in this land. But first take your father to a blind herbalist at Agavedo or you'll lose him," she said as she disappeared.

The next morning when he got up, he was hard put to remember all the instructions his mother's apparition had given him. But what he did remember, he set out to do immediately.

The spurious priest that morning was with his father doing his best to consult his gods to find some medications for him that day. He was very busy making incisions on Kwame's arm to implant herbs into his body when Afolabi entered and stopped the proceedings. He introduced himself to his ailing father as one of his sons but without detailing the circumstances surrounding his birth.

"I'm taking you to the hispital," he told his ailing father. His father's eyes glowed as life had suddenly entered him. With a big amazement from the spurious priest...

"Why? I'm treating him," objected the priest.

"No, you're not," Afolabi said, as he began to smoke marijuana to toughen himself against any opposition.

Seeing an unexpected threat to his livelihood, the priest rushed out to tell Kwame's senior wife of Afolabi's actions. They both rushed to try and stop Afolabi from removing his father to the hispital. By this time they all knew that Afolabi was a son also, for he resembled his father more than any of his brothers and sisters.

Their efforts were in vain, for Afolabi was not to be opposed and already had a rented car from town waiting. With the help of the driver, he removed his father from the sick bed, put him into the car, and took him to a nearby hospital. He did not take him to the blind herbalist his mother had mentioned because he had, quite simply, forgotten the instructions.

When they had left, both the household and the priest knew nothing would be the same when they returned. Part of the priest's payment was immediately given him.

A BURNING DESIRE

The family was afraid of Afolabi and alarmed by his rashness. They had never seen anyone act that way before. (Actually, Afolabi's rashness was entirely the product of a marijuana "high.")

A few hours after Afolabi had taken Kwame away, the priest packed and left. The house that had been a place of entertainment was now quietly subdued, as if the old man had already died. The children were quiet, not knowing where their father was.

A day later, the senior wife suggested to the others that she didn't think their husband would be coming home alive and that it might be best to call in their adult sons and daughters who lived in town for the distribution of the livestock. This suggestion was vehemently rejected by the youngest wife and the second. When the senior persisted, these two threatened to report the whole matter to the elders of the clan. This made the senior wife back off.

At all events, it was silly on her part to talk of distributing property when Kwame had not died yet. It was also against traditional law. Even if the old man should die, the elders would be the ones to distribute the property according to the number of wives he had, not according to the number of children he had. Seeing that she would be the loser, since she had many children, she was trying to outsmart them all.

At the hospital, at exactly twelve noon, his mother's apparition again appeared to Afolabi as he was dozing in a chair.

"Remove your father and take him to a blind herbalist at Agavedo. I know you forgot most of my instructions. I'll be working with you till your father feels better."

Afolabi got up suddenly. Remembering everything well this time, he lit a marijuana cigarette, smoked it, and with head spinning, went to the doctors and told them he would be taking his father away.

Coincidentally, the doctors themselves were going to release him for they had never seen a similar ailment and were unable to identify its cause. They released Kwame to him with good wishes.

Afolabi was not overjoyed at the prospect of having to be his father's keeper. He was not sure how much he could help the old man and his mother's apparition had already warned him to accept nothing from him. So there seemed no certainty of gain in it from either an altruistic or a purely selfish point of view. But what could he do? He would continue to help for now. After all he'd known that he wasn't alone at this time.

A BURNING DESIRE

Chapter VII

Afolabi hated the idea of taking his sick father to a voodoo priest. He had never had any contact with traditional healers. His aunt, Rebecca, had warned him to avoid visiting fetish homes.

With this fear of priests ingrained in him, he felt very apprehensive about this first visit. The exigencies of the situation had even made him forget, at least temporarily, about his dream of going to America.

He had no way of knowing that Joe Galas, his friend who was already there had not forgotten and was working on the papers he would need to get him there. The only difficulty Joe had was not knowing the whereabouts of Afolabi who had stopped writing him. Afolabi's last letter read this way:

July 2, 1980

Dear Joe,

It's very strange that since you left for America I haven't received a single letter or postcard from you. Remember, you promised to bring me to America.

The suffering in this country is no joke. Many are leaving for other parts of the world. I told you I don't have any family, no brothers, no sisters. I take you as my brother. I helped you so that once you were there it would be easy for me to join you.

I haven't been able to find anyone to get me a

41

visa. My money has also run out. I want to go to Nigeria, but I've been told too many people have gone there already and I'm afraid one day they may be shipped back. But I am seriously thinking about it.

For the present, I'm planning to go look for my father.

Adzoa has just died from a serious stomachache. You know how difficult it is to lose a woman this way. But what can I do? May she rest in peace. Perhaps one day I'll find a way to honor her memory more worthily. She was a beautiful woman to make love to and to love. I hope you share my sorrows and tears and that you will honor your promise by sending me the necessary documents to expedite my exit from this hot-hot land of Africa. Signed, sealed and to be delivered to a brother in heaven-USA.

Afolabi-the sorrowful, suffering boy left alone in this wide, wild, wonderous world of woefulness.

This was the letter that Joe Galas kept in his wallet, reading it repeatedly.

When Kwame and Afolabi journeyed to the village where the blind voodoo priest was, Afolabi was amazed at the sight of the huge legbas (idols) at the gate. He nearly ran away. But quickly a small wooden stick emerged from nowhere. The stick, about 12 inches tall and one inch in diameter, started to talk to him. "Your father is fine already," it said. The togbe (chief priest) came out of the voodoo house and approached them, but he was unable to persuade Afolabi to enter the shrine. He was very tall and heavily bearded. His chest was hairy and his big eyes were fully opened but blind.

He led Kwame inside where there were many people, some sick, others relatives of the sick. He had people helping him. His compound seemed to be a hospital. The only difference was that it had none of the instruments usually found in those places. His diagnostic instruments were hidden gods and different concoctions of herbs mounted in black pots.

After just two days, his father was completely cured. It was a big surprise to Afolabi. Following his cure, the chief priest explained what had caused his ailment.

It seems one of Kwame's wives had poisoned him. The soul of another wife, who had died many years ago, had intervened to save him for one reason only: that her son who had been neglected all these years, might be able to find him and have an inspiration in his life. If it had not been for Afolabi, Kwame would've died long before he visited him at his cattle ranch.

The chief priest knew it would have been just for Kwame to pacify both victims of his neglect, that is Afolabi and his dead mother. But he ordered the pacification of the soul of Afolabi's mother only, for tradition dictated that a father cannot kneel down before a child to beg his forgiveness.

They returned to the village in triumph. By this time most of his sons and daughters who had left before his ailment had returned when they heard of Afolabi's taking him away to an unknown destination. Some were very glad that someone unknown—their own half-brother had returned and taken care of their father. It was both a surprise and a mystery to all.

On the way home, Afolabi's father had promised to make him the head of his household.

"Whatever happened between your mother and me is all in the past,," he said. "I now know the real meaning of life. It was because of ignorance that I neglected your mother and you ever since you were born. "We're going to forge a new alliance. Education is very important. I never took it seriously before. You'll play a role in educating both your older and younger brothers and sisters. I promise you money is in the house. You've seen the number of cows on the ranch. If I must die, you should take all of them. I don't want them distributed among my children. That has been the practice for centuries and I think it only creates division among children. Since I've been ill, I've seen visions about the future of this wealth in the house. Before becoming ill, I had the same old ideas as everybody else about distributing it. And the wife whom I now suspect of poisoning me was suggesting that I start distributing it among my children, saying that I didn't know when I might die. I'm talking about my senior wife. Be very careful of her. Fortunately for me nd unfortunately for her, she had a lot of children for me and if sharing had to be by the tradi-tional way, she'd be the loser."

What's the traditional way?"

"That's sharing the inheritance according to the number of wives and not according to individual children. That's why she's against it," he told Afolabi.

His father seemed very distant to him. His inclination was to leave the country as soon as possible. But this new responsibility thrust on him by his father meant that he'd have to forget about going to America, at least for the time being. He did want some of Kwame's cows, for he could sell them right away for money to arrange his visa and ticket to the Land of Promise—the USA.

But he could not forget his mother's warning not to accept any form of gift from his father. Could his mother come to his aid in these difficult times?

The burden of accepting resposibility for everything after his father's passing and the family feud that was sure to follow were painful to contemplate. Without doubt his own mother would turn against him and even punish him severely if he did not try to heal this divided house. With all these pros and cons weighed, he decided to temporarily accept anything that his father might offer him. He would return to his aunt's house to tell the pastor what he went through. He would then make up his mind in which direction to go.

When Afolabi was about to depart, his father ordered two cows slaughtered. This made him delay his departure, for the old man wanted an opportunity to show his son his gratitude. Kwame had been made aware of many things hitherto unknown to him. The feast he proclaimed in his household was to celebrate the triumph of knowledge over ignorance, life over death, and most important of all, love over hatred.

To show Afolabi his love and repentance, he accompanied him to his aunt's house. But on the way, a mishap occurred. The car in which they were traveling collided with another automobile. Afolabi was the only one injured. He had his leg broken. Had it not been for the quick reflexes of the other driver, he'd have been killed.

With his father by his side, he's rushed in another car to the same voodoo priest who had aided in curing his father about a month ago. He had refused to enter this shrine before. Now he would've to.

His cure was simple. The chief priest took a chicken and broke its leg. He then applied similar herbal medication to both Afolabi and the chicken. As the chicken's leg healed, Afolabi's leg also healed.

This wasn't the first time the priest had used this method to cure broken legs that doctors had nearly amputated. Many school children playing soccer broke their legs and had to be brought from hospitals by angry parents whom the doctors had told that their children's legs had to be amputated. But the priest was able to heal them all.

Afolabi's mind now became more open to traditional ways. Just a few weeks earlier he had refused to enter the shrine to which he now owed his healing.

A BURNING DESIRE

Chapter VIII

Luck followed Joe Galas to America. Since arriving in New York, he had not had the difficulties experienced by other immigrants. He had gotten a job right away and been befriended by an African-American who was very interested in going to Africa to help in developing the continent.

Joe Galas, ambitious as he was, quickly convinced his new-found friend, Kudjo Obalewa, to open an African restaurant. The business was a great success. From the money accrued from the restaurant business, they opened another business -- a taxi service.

Obalewa was Africa-minded--Joe was not. He had made up his mind never to return to Africa. His hatred for Africa was so extreme that ever since arriving in New York, he had never written home to inquire about his relatives' condition. Kudjo Obalewa tried on many occasions to persuade him to change his mind but could not.

Joe had been through many untold hardships while in Africa and had given up on Africa. His attitude left Kudjo very confused and upset. While he understood Joe's concern for the total lack of certain things on the continent, he knew that forsaking Africa was obviously not the solution to the problem.

He discerned that Joe's problem was that he was miseducated. Kudjo tried to help him by inviting him to a series of lectures being delivered at a nearby church in Harlem by great African-American professors from American as well as Caribbean universities entitled FREEING YOUR AFRICAN MIND, but Joe was not interested.

Instead of blaming his own miseducation, Joe continued to blame African institutions. The more Kudjo tried to change his thinking, the more Joe ridiculed him and called him crazy.

One summer, Kudjo decided to go to Africa for vacation and study. They had made enough money to undertake the trip to Africa but Joe refused. Instead he went to Paris for his vaction. But before departing he rushed Afolabi's travel documents to him.

Referring to a recent letter, he managed to trace Afolabi's permanent residence. If there was anyone he dearly wanted to bring to America, it was Afolabi. He remembered Afolabi's kindness to him and wanted to help him. He decided to give Kudjo the documents to deliver to Afolabi personally. Kudjo was also to assist Afolabi if he needed any help. For the first time in many years, Joe Galas took a pen and wrote to someone in Africa.

June 30, 1982

Dear Afolabi,

I'm very happy you've finally found your daddy. Glad also that he had plenty of cows. But let me warn you before it's too late not to accept the idea of becoming the head of all his children and overseeing the cows. Or else you'll be mooing together with the cows in the grazing field or on the ranch before you know it. The moment your father dies, they'll be pulling your arms and legs to give them up. Don't ruely on any family property. Today I lost my father's cocoa plantations and coffee plantations, but I'm happy to be here and to be one of the few African arrivals who is doing well.

You know I like you and would like to help you out of that perpetual hell, that is unless you desire to become a future worshiper of cows, looking like bones stuck together, having no food to eat and starving together with those who are penniless. I'm telling you the truth. I've not written to you before, so I'm taking my time to detail everthing to you.

I'm going away for two weeks with my family, but will be back before you arrive. I've readied all the documents and a friend of mine will be delivering them to you and helping you any way he can. When you arrive here, don't worry. Everything you need I shall do it for you. As for a job, have no fears. I personally will give you a job.

Here you can become decent human being, enjoying the one life God put into you to enjoy before he calls you to eternity. Opportunity is abundant here and the sky, the blue sky, is the limit. If you don't mind working, you can make it like any successful person in America, not depending on your father, uncle, aunt or anyone. I, for one, don't think I shall ever return to Africa anymore. With that success, you can afford to eat any meat, drink any king of stuff you so desire.

I'm married to a white lady and we have four kids. They are all great kids and go to a good school. No worry about food for them as was the case back home.

49

A BURNING DESIRE

Books for kids to read even before kindergarten are all in the stores. Everything a human being can think of is in America. Medicine is no problem, music for relaxing--"beaucoup."

It's a pity our elected leaders couldn't provide us with our needs. Food is produced here around the clock, eaten up around the clock, and everybody jogs to lose weight and be healthy. We don't even produce enough in Africa to keep ourselves alive or be healthy. The only thing available back home is suffering, mourning, and crying for basic things a human being needs.

As Joe wrote this letter, he faintly heard an inner voice inside him advising and questioning: "who's to go to make all these possible"; but he paid no attention.

When you arrive in America, you'll see all these things for yourself. You'll see how people jog in the parks and on the sidewalks, lakesides, and riversides just to reduce their weight and be healthy. There's a style here to self-impose hunger to look attractive and shapely.

Don't delay. Hurry up before the gate is locked to those who may be late. Many from all over the world are pouring in. They're pouring in by boats by airplanes, by foot across all plains and terrains, lands, rivers and hot deserts.

Don't worry about clothes or pocket money. Your arrival is the most important thing.

Till I hear from you,

Your friend,
Joe Galas

A BURNING DESIRE

There was one person Afolabi's father wanted him to know and that was his uncle, his father's brother. He lived in his own village, nearby a fishpond he owned.

After visiting his aunt's house and meeting the pastor,they went to his uncle's village, a few miles from the bridge town.

On the way to his uncle's village, Afolabi informed his father of his desire to go to America, but his father had no enthusiasm for the idea.

"Whom do you know in that distant land?"

"I have friends over there," he assured him.

"It's not in my interest to see you go there."

"It's my desire to go. I've been trying hard for many years. But for lack of money I'm still here."

Kwame sighed in relief when he saw ripe pawpaw on a pawpaw-tree and insisted they should go and pluck it. It was ready to eat, but noone had plucked it. Not even the birds had taken a nibble. As they got closer, they discovered that many big, huge, succulent ones were quite ripe.

Afolabi's father, being an expert on how to shake the pawpaw trees and let them fall to the ground, got hold of the tree, and shook it. The pawpaws fell, among them a huge one that broke into many pieces. Kwame picked up one of the big ones, found the protruding root of a silk cotton tree and ordered his son to sit down. He sliced the appetizing pawpaw in two and gave Afolabi half.

"Wouldn't the owner be annoyed if he saw us eating his fruit without his knowledge?" he inquired.

"You think anyone owns it?" his father replied.

"It's for the birds. Nobody plants these fruits. Everybody is hungry, yet they wouldn't undertake the cultivation of these things.

"Imagine if we had pawpaw, banana, pear and plantain plantations and orange orchards covering every plot of land in this country. Do you think there would be hunger in the land and that everyone would be on the run to Nigeria or America?

"I told your older brothers we must undertake farming in conjunction with cattle rearing, but they didn't pay me any mind. See how old I am now. I've done my best. I've only a few years to live. The future is not going to be easy. A lot of people are being born and the demand for food will be great. "It's a good thing I brought you here and we came across this pawpaw. So think about it. Don't go to America. You've nobody there."

But Afolabi had already made his decision. He was sucking the juice of the pawpaw in absolute silence. His mind was far off.

"All right, let's go, son," his father commanded.

They started the journey carrying one of the biggest pawpaws for Afolabi's uncle. After walking a few miles, they arrived in a small hamlet that was as quiet as a cemetery. The old man welcomed them in.

"Have a seat," he said. He showed them to a long bench under a young coconut tree laden with very green coconuts. Then he brought them some water.

"This is Afolabi," said his father. "And this is your uncle Kwasi."

Afolabi got up to shake his uncle's hand and took

his seat again when Kwasi was settled with them.

"We humans are constantly making mistakes in life," the uncle began. "You're just like me," he said, addressing himself to his brother. "You know the woman I rejected as a young man because others ignorantly labeled her a whore could have given me children, instead of the one I stayed with all these years, thinking she would have baby until she died last year. Now here I am with no kids and too old to marry again. You've seen what your loving wife did to you, trying to kill you for your wealth. This boy's mother is the one you should've married. Then you would've enjoyed some peace. This child has suffered in life. You can read it in his face. He is not happy. You're lucky he hasn't become a vagabond since the death of his aunt.

"If you've anything to give him, give it to him now, before it's too late. I'd suggest you immediately open a new ranch for him. Or what do you plan for him?"

"I've informed him already," answered Afolabi's father.

"And what is it?" Kwasi demanded.

"To make him the leader of his brothers. He's educated and I think he can lead them well."

"What is wrong with you, my brother?"

"You think it's impossible, since they're older than him?'

"You know our tradition has no respect for being in school or being a scholar."

"Think of something better to tell him."

"What you said is possible. Just don't tell anyone you're opening the ranch for him. Build a small village for him. Let him get married and stay with his wife there in the village," agreed the uncle.

("Do they really think I'm going to spend my life in some village?" Afolabi thought, as they continued.)

"And it would automatically belong to him. Sounds good to me," concluded his father.

However, Afolabi himself wasn't in the mood to accept anything they were telling him. His mother's apparition had warned him to accept no gifts from them. His inclination was to get some money for a ticket and go to America. He was forgetting money constituted a gift also.

"Most of today's youths have no interest in farming. All they are interested in is going to America and bringing back cars a mile long, or going to Nigeria and bringing back those loud music-boxes, and hanging them around their shoulders, shaking their heads like Agama lizards," commented his uncle. Kwasi then got up and shook Afolabi's hand.

"Well, Nephew, it was nice meeting you. This is your one and only uncle here. Come visit me any time. This is your house. I've some history to tell you about our family."

"Okay, my brother. We shall be leaving."

"Nice of you to visit me. I shall be visiting you next week. And bring him another time, so that I can give him some herbs to protect himself."

Chapter IX

After his father's recuperation, Afolabi did not return to his aunt's house, where the pastor was staying, except to pick up his mail.

On one such visit, he received a strange letter from an unknown writer. The letter was puzzling, confusing and loaded with promises and advice. It had no date and no return address. It seemed to have arrived from the world of timelessness, and this is how it read:

"Dear Afolabi,

There's a land born out of the toil and sacrifice of millions. It's a beautiful land. You'll have the chance to go there soon. It's a glorious land, the hope of the future, and a country to be studied closely, it's good things copied. Bad ones thrown into the ocean, never to be retrieved.

You'll go there and meet many of your countrymen and women. Many are confused and worried about the suffering of the motherland today. You'll lead them to find solutions to problems, for if we can find answers to today's problems, we can solve tomorrow's as well. Help to build with ideas and never to criticize if you don't have any alternative ideas.

Of those who should be teachers, scholars, doctors, artists, scientists, mothers, fathers, farmers, many have left the motherland; this has contributed greatly to our problems. They've all gone because to sustain life presently is impossible for them. With all the knowledge acquired they never leant to turn their woes into wealth.

You'll acquire knowledge in the streets, the factories, in their transportation systems and in all their institutions. Know that the people of this great country have gone to the ants, the little termites in their homes, and learned from their way of doing things. They have studied the birds and made airplanes. They have studied whales and made submarines. They studied how ants made tunnels underground and they constructed their mass transport systems."

Here Afolabi burst into laughter. He was enjoying the letter. He wished he had the power to sprout wings and fly to that Promised Land right then and there. He continued reading:

"They came into our land and took away our simplest gadgets, modernized them, and mass-marketed them and gave jobs to their people. They took our religion and polished it and gave it back to us as theirs. Therefore continue to worship Jesus Christ or Allah, for they all teach you to practice what your own ancestors practiced at first. And know that if they tell you that you're a primitive worshiper, they're telling you you're the first worshiper. They learned from your motherland. You should go to America and learn again from them. Learn all the good things you can, the things that will help to give a meaningful life to your brothers and sisters back here in Africa.

"I know you'll surely become a true voice of the struggling land--the land of your ancestors.

"Don't bother to go to college. Just open your eyes and ears and most important of all your mind. The problems of your motherland can only be solved by the experiences gained from these places. Many want to go there like you. Many have already gone but have lain down and gone to sleep, even though it's not time yet for sleep.

"Many educated people today are suffering for they've been miseducated.

"You would never become a full independent human being if you grew up attached to your mother by the umbilical cord. For that reason, the cord is severed as soon as you're born. That's why I even left you early. Remember just 4 hours old. Afolabi gabed as his mother's ghost gave him some ideas about himself.

"Every living human being and living thing has something implanted in him naturally to direct him. Humans have the mind. Lower forms have instincts.

"Most lands are suffering today because they've gained their political independence, but they have refused to use or free their minds to do things for themselves. They still depend on their former colonisers for everything. They do not do basic things for themselves. What then is the meaning of independence? You grow up leave your parents, becoming independent. Who provides for your needs? Yourself?

"When you come to America, learn how they changed their way of doing things after becoming independent. The problems of the motherland today are a challenge to those with the ability to invent, to create and to supply the needs of others. The challenge is the demand of many, the suffering of many. If you can turn the many needs of your people around into a flowing supply, you have a job, an industry. You can be happy helping your people. And yourself as well. Preachers preach to church members to find salvation from living problems. They in turn make a living by preaching. Be eyes and ears.

Many will envy you or hate you but never mind them. Theirs is the way to unhappiness. God has given them minds so that they can become somebody and enjoy the fruits of their labor, but they've not used their God-given ability. Have you seen any human or animal without a head? That's why God put it there on the top--a head containing the mind to go sky high for happiness, to seek happiness everywhere, to mine gold and diamonds, to adorn, to sell, to make a living.

"You have to mine your latent talent to beautify yourself. Open your eyes; open your ears, open your heart to feel for others. And use your mind to supply their pressing needs. You'll be happy too. This is it," concluded the letter. It bore no signature. He finally knew the author of the letter. Surprised at the revelations inside it.

Afolabi read it over and over. He decided not to show it to anybody. He would keep it as a hidden treasure.

As he was about to depart for his father's village, some strangers came to the door. He thought they were looking for the pastor. When he ran to the door and opened it, he was amazed they were looking for him. He'd never seen anyone as tall as one of the visitors.

This man was heavily beared and very handsome. His intonation was music-like. He was a stranger from a strange land. He looked very healthy. He had no visible signs of suffering. Compared to his guides, there was a marked difference. They looked like people who had gone without food for months. Their ribs were like the accordion. They were people doomed to ignorant suffering unless their minds were changed and totally liberated, unless they liberated their African minds. These guides refused to do any job to make a living. But wasting time to depart to a foreign land as well.

"You can all have a seat here." He showed them some well-furnished living room sets, purchased moments after the pastor had moved into his aunt's house. Afolabi had sold the original room sets that Rebecca had bought to support his smoking and drinking habits.

"As tradition goes, you as well as your spirits-souls must all drink first before your mission to our house is demanded," as Afolabi bagan to turn to traditional rites slowly.

"Is this not a pastor's residence?' questioned one of the guides, as the water was served round and he poured some down as libation.

"Yes, but he doesn't condone all aspects of our culture," answered Afolabi smiling.

"Ha, ha, ha, ha. He doesn't condone it all," the tall and bearded strange-looking man broke up with a rich laughter.

"Well, you're all welcome. My name is Afolabi," he introduced himself.

"Call me Kudjo Obalewa," the tall man introduced himself.

The two guides did the same.

"Are you from Nigeria?" Afolabi asked the tall one.

"No. Why?

"I wanted to know if you come from Nigeria because my own ancestors come from Nigeria."

"Well, I know one thing for sure--that all black people made their exodus from the Nile Valley due to a population explosion and other factors, and came through old Ghana, Niger, and Nigeria towards the ocean. Sone continued to other areas, namely present-day Ghana, Nigeria, Zimbabwe, Azania and many other countries and most recently of all, to my place of exile--America. So our roots are all over the continent. You're not wrong in asking if I come from Nigeria or not. We Africans can all be Nigerians, Ghanaians, Zimbabweans, Azanians, Sudanese or Ugandans. But to end all these divide-and-conquer terms, the most important thing we should know is that we are Africans. Jews in Israel are Jews. Jews in Poland are Jews. Jews in Russia are Jews. Jews in Spain, Morocco, Britain, America, Azania, or Namibia are Jews. The most important thing is the race--the African race and I categorically reject the name black as well as regional names designed to suit aliens. I'm glad you asked such a beautiful question, a question that united us all at one blow," he said, terminating the long lecture that had never been heard by these young brothers of his.

"So you're from America?" Afolabi inquired.

"Yes. Do you think you would like the place?" Kudjo then reached for his leather shoulder bag and pulled out a parcel for Afolabi.

Afolabi got up and dashed to the refrigerator and brought out some bottles of beer the pastor had left.

He returned and apologized for his forgetfulness. He said his mind was far away from the house.

"Your mind was in America, ha?" Kudjo questioned jokingly. Kudjo seemed to be a man of great fun. He could make you forget about your worries and debts with his rich laughter.

"Here, this parcel is for you--from an old friend of yours."

Afolabi reached for the parcel and retired to another room to read the letter inside. Soon he was called back.

"May we know if we can find accommodation with you?" Kudjo asked as if speaking for everyone. "You know I'm not a stranger. I'm at home in my Africa," he said with confidence.

"Sure you're at home. You're all welcome to stay."

As it turned out, the guides decided to return to their homes, so, of course, Kudjo was Afolabi's sole guest. It was he who paid the guides who, bowing many times in gratitude, departed.

Afolabi again retired to the den so he could finish reading the letter in solitude. The letter was from his old friend Joe Galas and what it said made him sweat and tremble with excitement: Kudjo would be helping him with the needed documents and he would be coming to America! Joe had everything ready for him. He returned to the living room, smiling radiantly.

Kudjo then livened things up with more of his humor and entertainment.

"You've some good news for me or only for yourself?"

"Only for me. All my troubles seem to have

vanished today," he said enthusiastically.

"If you believe so, that's a good sign."

Afolabi started to shake his head disbelievingly. For the first time in his entire life, he envisioned a positive future.

Now that there would be no need for his father's gifts, he wouldn't have to be the leader of the family. The other brothers' jealousies had been avoided also. And greatest of all was the fulfillment of a long overdue promise by Joe Galas whom he'd given up hope on. He'd proved in the long run to be a true, dependable friend. His letter was the most interesting he had ever received from a friend. Not even those teenage love letters he had exchanged with Beatrice with "I love you 99-3/4%. You add only the remaining 1/4% to make it 100%," were more thrilling.

This day he would never forget.

The next morning they worked on strategy. Afolabi was exceptionally happy. Visa, the number one problem that kept many from reaching America, had been solved. He was so pleased his friend had taken care of this important detail for him.

"We grow many crops but harvest very few," he said, making allusion to the fact that he had helped many but didn't get any reward from them.

"What's your next move?"

"My next move is to fly away. No, no, no. I've got to go bid the elders goodbye," he said with a laugh.

"Won't there be a confrontation?"

"No, it's c-o-o-l," Afolabi replied, confiding in his ability to deal with any objection.

A BURNING DESIRE

"I've got to plan very carefully what to tell them. But if they should raise any objection, I'd just ignore them."

"Ignore your parents? You sound like a New Yorker already."

"My father is kind of c-o-o-l, but an uncle I visited a few days ago looked like a tough person."

"What about your mother?"

"She passed away a long time ago. It's a long story, very long," he said.

"Can we market that story?"

"Market it how?"

"You write the story in the form of a book and we sell it."

"I don't believe I can write a book."

"Hey, don't say that! Everything's possible. You have an uncle who knows family stories dating very far back, don't you?"

"This uncle I just met seemed to. My father was telling me he's the historian, the philosopher of our family. "He invited me to come visit him but I refused. I was told by my brothers, "If you visit him, he'll send you to a distant place to get him tobacco. When you return, he'll then be recounting ancient battles fought by our ancestors in defence of our stool lands against enemies, including whites, as you struggle with the tobaccogrinder." "One of his famous battle memories is the Sagbadre War. This war, according to him, was fought and won by our ancestors when, upon their chief commander's orders, small birds called Sagbadre descended and consumed all the bullets the white soldiers fired." "That's quite heavy. I'd like to meet him. He's my man." Kudjo was indeed in Africa to learn and give his mind a rest from the pressures of big city life. "How old is your uncle?" he inquired.

"Who knows? He said he was that tall when the first earthquake in recent memory took place," he said, indicating his uncle's height at that moment. And judging by that height, considering all nourishment factors together with the actual date of that severe earthquake, he must by 70-plus now.

"One thing he also used to tell my brothers about was his younger brother's fighting alongside the British in Burma in the Second World War. He didn't like the idea at all. Why should a black man fight for a white man in such a far-off place when he hasn't even won the battle for himself where he is?"

"That's time."

The things his brother recounted to him upon his return from the war, he still used to talk about, namely heavy rains, huge mosquitoes and malaria. It was these that hastened his death soon after he was home. "I'd like to see him" Kudjo sighed. He identified with the old man's views about the war.

"Afolabi, however, wasn't too pleased about going to his uncle's house with Obalewas. Not until he had everything firmly in hand.

"Your uncle should have been a lecturer instead of those expatriates brought from abroad to teach history and other things. His stories should have been part of the novels or history books being used in the schools and colleges. If that had been done, there wouldn't be so much suffering on the continent today. Importing books from overseas together with foreign teachers will always brainwash and miseducate youths to leave this precious -expanse of land.

"That's true replied Afolabi."

"This land could've been developed so that food would be plentifully available. But when I visited the libraries, the books were all from outside. Why should kids be reading and learning about apples, peaches, plums strawberries, wheat, and a host of other crops that can't be grown on this continent? Why not pineapple, oranges, cassava, yam, potatoes, maize, and other things which are native to the soil, the African soil?" Kudjo had become a true modern-day missionary with African Bible in hand.

"It's true we have to eat what we grow." "We also have to read what we write and what our ancestors did in the past," Afolabi added. "But who will start the movement?" he questioned.

"You," Kudjo answered.

"Me? I'm not qualified," Afolabi said unbelievingly.

"You see there is a reason for everything they do. By using the educational process to direct our young people's attention and interest towards their books, their crops, and their way of life the whites have succeded in opening up avenues to market their products here and everywhere. And what are the results of this policy here in Africa? Our people lose interest in cultivating their own crops, publishing their own books, and maintaing their own tradition. I'll bet you know more about the world outside Africa than the world inside Mother Africa," he said to Afolabi.

"That's true."

"You know the names of more cities in America than you do in Africa. Don't you?" You know when Columbus set sail from Spain. But not when our ancestors started moving from the Nile River Basin?

Afolabi nodded in affirmation and negation respectively for the heart throbbing question.

Afolabi wasn't experienced about life in general. What Kudjo was talking about was beyond him. But Mr. Obalewa was quite genuinely concerned about the westernization and europeanization of his dear Africa which had brought about the loss of physical and mental power in African. He had seen too many African students caught up in very unproductive fields in America. He had met some and discussed the situation in Africa with them. He urged them to return to the motherland and help, but most of them didn't know the area where they would fit in. They complained there weren't any jobs. They refused to believe that the lacks of the continent were "resources" for them to use. If only they knew that the jobs they wanted so desperately were inside themselves. Demand creates provision. Provision satisfied wants. How could one become a Business Administrator when there was no business to adminster?

Afolabi didn't want to introduce Kudjo to his elders, especially his uncle, until he had secured all his documents. He made this decision on the grounds that if his elders refused to accept his decision and

Kudjo also gave in, he would be the one to suffer.

Early in the morning of the third day since Kudjo arrived they departed for the Consular Office in the city.

With absolute ease, he received his visa. He could see frustration, depression and misery in the faces of many rejected applicants. They could all have used a friend like Kujdo to help them.

Afolabi had helped his friend Joe greatly. He had sheltered him, provided him with clothes, money for the movies--even money for women--and most important of all his plane ticket. So he was glad Joe was finally paying him back.

What Joe had done made good friendship to triumph. In his palm were the things he had wished, desired, dreamed about, hoped and longed for all the years since he had lost his aunt and found his father.

With ticket, visa, and foreign exhange in his hand, he decided to enter the world of girls and drinks for a-while.

After safely securing his documents in an old friend's home, he took lodging at a hotel. Kudjo had gone to do some sightseeing in other cities of the country and promised to return to his elders in a few days.

While Afolabi was making up for lost time in the city, he met an old acquaintance who knew him as Adzoa's boyfriend. After finding out where Afolabi lived, he went and reported Afolabi's whereabouts to her bereaved family.

But Afolabi had already had his suspicions about this "friend," so he moved out and took lodging in another hotel. Luckily for him, and unluckily for the bereaved family, he missed them.

He knew how vicious some families were from his first experience with Beatrice and the subsequent kidnaping attempt many years back. Because of this he didn't leave any note for Kudjo at the first hotel. He knew if Kudjo returned and didn't see him he would simply come to his home town. And that is exactly what Kudjo did.

When Kudjo heard Afolabi's story, he advised him not to delay his departure for America. Therefore, Kudjo did not have the chance to meet his uncle, but upon Afolabi's insistence, he went and saw his father.

Afolabi's family received the news of his plans to leave for America without enthusiasm. His father felt expecially hurt, because he had made plans to transfer some of the cows to a new ranch to be built for Afolabi. But, as it was, he had to shelve all those plans. The old man was very unhappy because since his return from the sick-bed to active life, some of the animals had mysteriously vanished. He din't know where they were. Therefore, his brother's idea of making a new ranch had come as a blessing for him, only to be frustrated by his son.

The year Afolabi was departing, many who had already gone were returning home as "been-tos." They brought a host of troubles in their wake. The "been-tos" sported Posh cars, televisions, video-cassettes, and expensive clothes. Some were taking wives away from their husbands with their false promises, others were swindling people out of their money by the same means, and still others were getting naive young girls pregnant.

The girl-victims were being left behind to struggle with infants they had little to take care of with.

Afolabi and Kudjo saw some "been-tos" drinking beer with girls at the airport where Kudjo had come to see him off.

"Look at these 'been-tos' very carefully and don't come back acting like them," advised Kudjo.

Afolabi was very familiar with their attitudes so the statement needed no detailing.

The airport that morning was jammed with travelers. Some were leaving. Others had come to see loved ones off.

Afolabi had been in such a rush to get to the airport that he had taken no breakfast that morning. They decided to go in and have some hot cocoa at the cafe.

Just as they sat down to give their order, Afolabi spotted a former girl friend passing by. It looked like she was desperately looking for someone. However, he made no attempt to attract her attention.

"Look, that's one of my girls," he whispered into Kudjo's ears.

"Oh, she's fine. Are you going to send for any of them later?"

"Ah, there are plenty of women in America," said Afolabi.

A BURNING DESIRE

"How do you know?" his friend asked.

"Ah, we've been seeing the movies and the magazines. I'm especially interested in the white thighs."

"What? What's the African world coming to? Every notable African wants to go with a white woman and not his own."

Afolabi started to laugh. "I'm only joking. My African wife came to America long ago with my unborn baby. She must have had the baby by this time."

In the meantime, the ex-girl friend continued her impatient search. She had sunglasses in her left hand. It seems she had just heard from another friend that he was leaving. To tease her, the friend added a false detail: Afolabi was planning to send for one of her rivals as soon as he arrived in America. This false intelligence so angered her that she had decided to come to the airport and poison him.

Afolabi and Kudjo finished their cocoa and as they were leaving, she spotted them. She ran to Afolabi smiling.

Why? why? why? you're leaving and you didn't bother to inform me?"

Afolabi did not answer her.

She invited them back to the cafe' for a drink, but they turned her down. She then went and sat down at a table with two men. They had had plenty of bear already and were wearing heavy overcoats. With the temperature that early morning above eighty degrees, there was hardly any need for such, but here these two ignorant men were wrapped up in winter coats! Afolabi and Kudjo decided it would be beneath their dignity to join them.

"Let's go and have the last one for the road," she insisted.

"Perhaps, the last one into eternity," he said as though he's a psychic to Obalewa.

They again refused her offer. Since they were unyielding, one of the intoxicated fools dressed in the winter coat dashed to them and introduced himself to them as her cousin.

"Hey, don't disgrace my cousin. She's happy to see you gonna go to the Promised Land. Let's go have a drink before you slash out, Afro," he said, using his own version of American slang.

"America has taken deep root in here," Kudjo joked. "We all love America. But I think we are loving her wrongly. What we should be doing is studying how she learned to do the impossible things that have contributed to making life easy for so many. But wearing a winter coat in ninety- degree temperature is positively un-American," he concluded on a somewhat sterner note.

By this time the intercom was calling for all passengers to start boarding.

Afolabi suddenly felt a shiver through his entire body. It was the final hour, the departing hour. When he looked back his former girl friend and the two ignorants were nowhere to be found. At least he wanted to bid them goodbye. But the girl as a result of the failure of her plans, left the scene without notice.

"Passengers for Lagos, Frankfurt and New York are boarding," came the announcement once more.

Kudjo shoke his hand and said, "God be with you

throughout the journey. Tell Joe I'll be arriving soon"

Afolabi went through the check point. Kudjo bid him a final "adios." Afolabi waved his last goodbye and boarded the plane.

Suddenly his mother's ghost appeared with a message: "Young man, you're lucky. A girl just nearly poisoned you. So be very careful of girls from now on. Your love is there waiting -- seek her." That was all and she was gone.

Undoubtedly he was right in his "psychic world".

"No doubt the angels are protecting me and my mother is still with me," Afolabi soliloquized, as he waited for the Lufthanza to take off.

He knew he would miss Africa, but not her harsh, difficult life.

En route to Frankfurt from Lagos International Airport, he overhead two men discussing Nigeria.

"This country has something the world market demands."

"What's that?" the other asked.

"Oil. Many international buyers and workers are pouring in."

"Yeah, we're pumping it to them and they are just storing it underground for future drilling. And when our own supply is depleted and we go back to them for oil, we shall have to trade our independence for it," remarked the second man.

Afolabi knew these two gentlemen were talking Nigerian nationalism.

"They should meet Kudjo Obalewa," he thought to himself.

A BURNING DESIRE

En route, Afolabi thought about how lacking in resourcefulness and creativity Africans born on the continent had become. He said to himself, "Instead of the creation of industries, factories and services, what many have contributed is businesses in briefcases, and fancy offices serving as international agencies only.

"You go to the banks -- there is no foreign exchange. The stores are empty. Foreign goods take too long to arrive. Nothing is being locally made.

"So-called businessmen and corrupt politicians have been misusing money alloted them to import essentials for the country, chanelling it into the black market economy instead. And opening bank accounts in foreign lands. The poor tax-payers and their children suffer for all these.

"The universities don't support any practical endeavors. Students graduating are practically ignorant as those who haven't been to school at all. Everything studied in these institutions has no meaning as soon as the graduates leave the schools and face life outside. Their degrees and diplomas are becoming more and more living room decoration only."

As the plane flew sky-high his mind was totally inundated with the woes of his departing motherland.

A BURNING DESIRE

Chapter X

Joe Galas and his white American wife, Carol, had just returned from four weeks' vacation in Paris. Unfortunately, while they were vacationing in France, a misunderstanding developed between them. His wife nearly cut short her stay on account of it. However, to give her temper a chance to cool down, she moved from their Hotel Parisienne suite to another one by herself in the Hotel d'Ivoire and they did come back to New York City together.

But no sooner had they dropped their bags than Carol filed for a divorce. At first, Joe couldn't believe it -- he thought she would change her mind. He had never thought in terms of a divorce, or even a separation. What about their children? If separation should take place, he knew the children would suffer.

He tried very hard to win back his wife.

"Look, Honey. I love you. We both have invested too much time and energy in this relationship to let it go down the drain over a very minor misunderstanding."

"Why don't you ever try to understand what I want? We could've gone without this developing into any misunderstanding," she retorted.

"You know I dislike those obscene films. It's against my culture. I know your culture permits things of that nature. But I've tradition to keep. Although I have spoken unfavorably about Africa on many occasions, I can't give in to a lifestyle that is against my dignity as an African."

74

A BURNING DESIRE

"When do I ever ask you to take me to such movies in New York? I really don't care about them. But the trip to Paris was a once-in-a-lifetime event. I wanted to be able to say to my friends when I got back to New York, 'You know that film that was banned in New York City and every city in America? Well, I saw it in Paris on my vacation!' You hurt my feelings and nothing can remedy that humiliation."

Joe was very much worried. If this marriage should fail, he would have to start all over again. He had made a terrible mistake by letting all of their property bear only his wife's signature. Now he couldn't claim anything even partially. The cars, the two-family house, and the money in the bank all were in his wife's name. Now everything he'd worked so hard for in America all these years seemed about to go "down the drain."

He began to contemplate his life. He was very sorry he had made that trip to France. He felt equally guilty that he had cursed his motherland. He began to suspect supersititiously that such ungrateful curses might have contributed to the disaster that now appeared imminent.

He had enjoyed a very comfortable life since marrying this white woman. Would he have been better off marrying a lady of his own race? His mind repudiated that suggestion. His own race had been hard hit with divorce and separation, he rationalized. Would he have been better off had he taken his wife on a safari? Perhaps he would have. Would that visit not benefit Africa? At least it would bring a few tourist dollars to Africa.

Thinking of the good times past, he became very frustrated. Where was he heading now? After cursing Africa in the past, he now felt very much in love with her, especially her traditional institutions. He wished he were in Africa where a woman couldn't just file for a divorce and take away everything that belonged to a family. In Africa, he would of course be the master. The house and the children would automatically be his. The time had now come for him to value some of the traditions of his motherland. Now he would need permission from the white man's court to visit his own children.

"American men are being driven crazy by the laws that favor their women only. These laws are no good," he observed.

He had a friend who had had to move out of a beautiful house in Mount Vernon in the wake of a divorce. He decided to go to him and seek some brotherly advice.

"My brother, I'm in the soup. I'm being fried," he said and burst out laughing.

"What do you mean?"

"I lost my house, my money, and my children."

"What? Was there a fire in your house?" panicked his friend.

"Would I be laughing about it if I'd lost everything and everybody in a fire?"

"Well, it's possible. Maybe your tear glands refused to respond and your laughing glands took over instead," he joked.

"My wife has divorced me and taken the bank accounts. And the kids -- forget it. All I've got now is visitation rights.

"But you just returned from a gorgeous exhilarating vacation in Paris. Pourquoi toutes ces difficultes? Parce que vous ne parlez pas francais? Ou couchez-vous avec mademoiselle la difference?" he said, teasing him in French.

"I came to you for advice. Never mind the 'couchez-vous'"

"Talk to her again. Offer to take her on a cruise on the Pacific Ocean -- that's a cooling, pacifying ocean, his friend continued teasingly. "If you marry a white woman, you've got to do the things they ask for," he said, finally coming through with one solid bit of advice.

All Joe's friends had heard about the trip to Paris and most of them were not pleased with the news. Joe's mother was sick, and although the family had sent him many a cable about her condition, he had never bothered to go and visit her. Instead, he had taken his wife on an exotic vacation to Paris. Rather than travel to Africa to see his mother, he preferred to send people with money to go and see her.

Joe felt like he was being punished for his ungratefulness to his own mother and family in Africa. He had foresaken his African family and taken to his white family.

Joe's African friends didn't like the way he was treating his own parents and brothers. For his part, he always claimed they had treated him very badly while he was growing up and while he was going to college in Africa. Still, they would always be there for him. He no longer had any such certainty about his white family.

A BURNING DESIRE

Joe felt like he was losing on all fronts. Soon Afolabi would arrive and meet him without even a home.

Afolabi would be the most victimized of all. He needed someone to direct him as soon as he landed in the city. Now even to meet him at the airport would be a problem. Joe had no peace of mind. He wished he hadn't ever sent for Afolabi in the first place. Now he regretted the beautiful, thoughtful letter he had written him. But it was too late. Afolabi was en route and soon would be landing.

Since the divorce papers had been signed, Joe had been living with one of his drivers. The fact that he was no longer a white woman's husband had demeaned him so much in their eyes that his drivers had started to render wrong accounts on the cars he personally owned with Kudjo Obalewa.

The influence he had enjoyed married to a white woman had started to evaporate -- and fast!

In twenty-four hours Afolabi would be landing. He would have to go and meet him at the airport.

In anticipation of Afolabi's arrival, Joe had renewed communication with his ex-wife. He had also started to exercise his visitation rights, without problem.

In addition, he asked Carol to let Afolabi stay in the visitor's room. (Joe had no space in his rooming house). She raised no objection.

Furthermore, to his happy surprise, Joe also had gotten Carol's permission to use the luxurious Mercedes Benz 540 SE, to pick Afolabi up.

He indeed missed their beautiful evening dinners, the weekend drives through town, and the ballroom dances. He was very sorry to have ruined his marriage by being too "macho."

This tendency he blamed on his bad temper. Joe Galas, being a Leo, was very stubborn. Unless he learned the art of compromise, life would always be hard for him.

Many of his friends advised him to go and talk once more to Carol. After all, she had given everything he had asked for on behalf of Afolabi. Maybe if he spoke for himself. So back he went but Carol refused his apology. She had not wanted to make them both look bad by resufing hospitality to his friend, but neither had she any interest in reconciling with him.

Meanwhile, en route to JFK Airport, the two Nigerians and Afolabi had been discussing Africa in general and Nigerian in particular.

"I've heard rumors, from the highest echelons of government that in a few years' time, all illegal aliens will be deported," said one Nigerian. "I've heard that from reliable sources, too," the other added.

"Millions would be involved," suggested Afolabi.

"Well, our people have been sent away and discriminated against by other nations. It's time for us to act," said one of the Nigerians.

"But it must be done humanely," suggested Afolabi. "Our people have never been humanely treated by others," the first Nigerian reminded him.

"Leaders of Africa should learn that an African living on any part of African soil must be considered to be at home and not an 'alien.' The same protection accorded people born there must be extended to him as well," said the second Nigerian.

A BURNING DESIRE

"Shake my hand," Afolabi agreed. "National bound- aries are the white man's idea. He put these lines on the map, imaginary lines here and there, dividing our people and he enjoyed the benefit of it in the past, and is enjoying it now by his divide-and-conquer prac- tices of which we Africans are the perpetual victims. These boundary lines turn nation against nation and their people against one another. Who gains in the long run? The white man. And who loses? The very people split into pieces by invisible lines. If this happens, I hope my country will take it as a matter between brothers that must be resolved amicably. We need a strong Nigeria, a strong Ghana, and a strong Zimbabwe to lead towards a strong Africa that will be able to keep all aliens and their unwanted ideas out," concluded Afolabi.

If African people are treating their race - African race, this way, how can the world react to the treatment of our Azania Brothers in South Africa without rediculing us. As that beautiful land of Africa is overtaken and our brothers and sisters physically and sentiment- ally subjected to "technological slavery." Everything done to Africa people in the past continent-wide is being perpetrated there everyday. The split ups, racial frontiers, you name it. You have it. The pain, the yearning, I want O.A.U. to speak out. New ideas must be instituted for Mother Africa's desperate children. You and me, our brothers, our sisters, our children. They must be free on their own soil. No boundaries. No frontiers to cross fearlessly, painfully or sorrow- fully. Africa, Africa, Africa. I'm calling you. Move act, double up. Redecorate. One, strong, productive and smiling Africa. A burning desire," he concluded.

Many whites sitting nearby gabed and listened. Heads turned. Eyes closed "day dreamingly". "A new voice for Africa", they wondered.

It wasn't too long before the loudspeaker announced they would soon be landing at JFK. In the twinkle of an eye, they were taxiing on the ground.

Afolabi was in America. He got up and joined the lines of others about to disembark, carrying his small traveling bag with him.

He passed through customs without incident and came out to the bag collection area. He saw his bag going around. Patiently, he waited and when it came to where he was standing, he grabbed it and went to the inspection section. They allowed him to pass without searching him. His friends from Nigeria wanted to give him a ride home but he politely refused -- he wanted Joe Galas to have that honor.

Things had not gone well for Afolabi back in Africa since Joe's departure. He had lost a lot of weight. He wondered if Joe would recognize him. To hide his deep-set eye sockets, he was wearing sunglasses.

He was a man standing with his elbows resting on a Mercedes Benz, but he didn't realize that it was Joe.

Joe didn't recognize him either, both because of the dark glasses and because his mind was far away thinking about his domestic problems.

At first, Afolabi was so enthralled at New York's skyscrapers that he almost forgot about finding his friend. But his mind soon returned to this purpose and his eyes scanned the airport in search of him. He became anxious when he didn't see him. Then he calmed himself and focused his concentration.

He looked around him. The man with the Mercedez Benz was still standing there. He could see that he was also very anxious about finding someone.

"Two negatives make a positive; let me approach him," he said to himself.

He took off his sunglasses as he approached him. "Joe!" he yelled. "Can't you see me?"

"Hey, my brother. You're the one I was looking at all the time. Didn't you see me?" Joe said, as they hugged each other.

"Welcome, welcome. This is America. Welcome to the USA," said Joe, forgetting his own problems momentarily.

"Hey, this is your car? You should be President. With this car, I'll vote you to rule the people. But look at your hair -- you changed it from big 'Afro' to Jerry curl. You're looking great. Oh, how happy I am to see you! America is good for you," Afolabi said as he continued to admire his friend.

Joe couldn't believe the physical appearance of his friend.

"Afolabi, you look very small and thin. Are you sick? May I take you to the hospital. You look very sick."

"You know something, I'm not sick. But if I go to the hospital, the doctors will certainly find something. I don't want to go - not just now."

"No, no, no. I must take you to the hospital."

"Don't worry, I'm quite well, but I'm just thinking because there was not much to eat in Africa. "The past civilian governments have dried the nation's savings and ignorantly fatten the foreign accounts". The new government is trying but the foreign governments have refused to help." You can't get three meals a day any more. And you know our parents, the ones with cows, they won't slaughter them for meals either. It's a long story."

"Get inside the car," Joe told him. He was overwhelmed with sadness at Afolabi's physical condition. It reminded him painfully of the hunger situation in Africa.

They started out from the airport and took the highway to Manhattan. Afolabi, despite his poor physical condition, was in high spirits. His mood was lively.

Joe frantically searched for a good music station on the radio. He found one that was playing an old song that went like this:

> Oh, Carol, I'm but a fool.
>
> You treat me bad and make me cry.
>
> Don't leave me,
>
> You will hurt me
>
> And make me cry.
>
> I still love you.
>
> 'Cause I love you,
>
> If you leave me, I'll die.

Joe tried to change the station but Afolabi protested. So he let it remain. He felt hurt because it reminded him of his wife.

A BURNING DESIRE

"That's a beautiful song. Don't you remember the good old days any more?" querried Afolabi who was very happy to meet his friend and be taking a jolly ride through New York City to his house. They continued the beautiful ride while they listened to more songs.

Joe tried very hard to hide his pain and talked amicably with Afolabi as they drove home.

Driving through the city of New York really excited Afolabi. From far and near, the skyscrapers could be seen. Numerous cars, buses, and limousines cruised past them very smoothly and many could likewise be seen speeding across the bridges.

They were floating in a sea of cars of all sizes. As they approached LaGuardia Airport, they started singing another famous old song:

> Baby, you don't know
> how to love somebody.
> Baby, you don't know
> how to love somebody.
> I see your face again--
> You ain't got to be so bad.
> You can't see what I am.
> I'll do everything for you
> If I can get you.
> Baby, baby, you don't know
> What it is life
> To love somebody
> To love somebody
> The way I love you.

Joe wished he were driving together with Carol, for all the beautiful songs could have helped them settle their old quarrel.

Afolabi was so delighted. He hadn't heard those songs in years.

"Is that a second JFK?" Afolabi inquired.

"No, that's Laguardia Airport, serving internally only."

"It's just as big," observed Afolabi. "They don't think small. They think big every time," he joked.

"Look at the limousine wheeling past us. It even has a cocktail bar inside, telephones as well. Look at how the couple inside are enjoying. Oh, great Almighty! This is life. This is happiness. This is heaven and most of all paradise. You think there is another paradise anywhere?" he questiuoned, as they both laughed.

"You ain't seen nothin' yet," Joe answered.

"You'll soon be americanized."

"No, I'll be returning in a couple of years."

"That's what a lot of people have said, when first arriving but they've been here now for two decades--and more. People came here together with our founding fathers--Dr. Kwame Nkrumah, Dr. Nnamdi Azikiwe, Dr. Siaka Stevens and many others from Africa, but still haven't returned. That's why I said, 'You haven't seen anything yet.' If I were to tell you something right now--" he stopped short. "I don't want to frighten you."

The ride continued in silence until they were in front of the house.

Carol looked down from the window and saw them. She went back inside. Perhaps she had been worried about the car.

A BURNING DESIRE

As they stood outside talking about Afolabi's luggage, which was still at the airport, she came downstairs to meet them. On hearing that Afolabi had lost his luggage, she tried to console him.

When they had settled down a bit, they began to talk of other things, like African identity.

"Dashikis don't make you an African--the most important thing is your African mind," Carol contributed.

"Oh, that's a beautiful, wise, intelligent statement," said Afolabi. "You're a beautiful wife, a very smart woman. You have been blessed. In addition to this gorgeous home and luxurious car, on top of it all is a beautiful wife and handsome kids. God bless both of you. Your heads must be together. The world is small. We are all the same. Coming from the same roots--black or white. We must unite. Black and white must unite. For only then can a harmonious sound emerge from both the black and white keys to be enjoyed by the world. A world without music would be a boring world," he said to the divorced couple.

His words had such an effect on both of them that they excused themselves.

When they came back, Joe had a real smile on his face for the first time.

"The bag that got lost at the airport contained my troubles. It was my troubles that got lost. Thank you, Afolabi. You brought happiness to my house," he whispered into his ear.

Afolabi somehow sensed what the remark meant without explanation.

A BURNING DESIRE

Chapter XI

The job situation in the United States at the time Afolabi arrived was very bleak. Many people were without jobs. Legislative leaders blamed lack of jobs on illegal immigrants. While some Americans agreed with the legislators, others defended the immigrants' right to be in the country.

Finding a job had not only become very difficult, but also very risky. The Immigration officials were empowered to arrest aliens and deport them. The alien community was in perpetual fear. Many had to change from day to night shifts to escape arrest.

They had become the scapegoats of American politics. A nation which had been built by immigrants over the centuries was caught unprepared for these modern immigrants. They were now being called unwanted aliens. Those who came for opportunity unlimited were being shown the exit door. The meaning of the Statue of Liberty is now forgotten. It isn't there to beckon and welcome any more--it is now a museum for visitors to come and see. The once-loved symbol of liberty has simply become a thing of the past.

Since his arrival, Afolabi had shown marked physical improvement. He had gained weight rapidly and started to enjoy New York City life. Instead of water, he now had orange juice for breakfast, drank fresh milk, and took three meals a day.

When he first arrived in New York, he had to be coaxed to eat. He was very shy and bashful. When it was time for dinner, he wouldn't come to the table but would be crying.

A BURNING DESIRE

When he was asked the reason for his strange behavior, he said he was sorry for the brothers in his country who couldn't even get a quarter of what he was being served daily.

"You'd better take care of yourself right now. If you start worrying about your brothers, you won't achieve anything for yourself or for them," advised Joe.

"Eat and be strong and think of ways and means at your disposal to help them out of their predicament," added Carol.

Two weeks after his arrival, his uncle, the self-proclaimed historian, had died. This information was relayed to them by Kudjo. He had gone to see him and had a lenghty talk with him before he died.

In a special letter to Afolabi, he described the uncle as a walking library. In that same letter, Afolabi learned that his dead uncle had bequeathed to him a very huge lake with fishes.

His uncle's death saddened him, but he tried very hard to forget it.

Afolabi was with the Galas' for a long time.

At Christmas time, he got a nice present from them. Two things had made them decide to give Afolabi this rather expensive gift. The first was the help he had given Joe in Africa. The second was the luck he brought into their home. Because of his presence, their marriage had been restored. The gift was a new automobile. It was a very joyous occasion when the keys were presented to him. Among all the friends he had helped, Joe was the one who had paid him back the most handsomely.

To help him get his bearings, Joe showed him how to operate a taxi and gave him one of the company taxis to drive.

Joe also gave him generous terms so that he could save fast to have his own taxi. Instead of weekly accounting of $125 which applied to all the other drivers, Afolabi was required to bring in only $75.

Joe did this to help him save for the future.

As Afolabi started meeting others in the business, he began to change.

It wasn't long before he couldn't account for even a dollar a week. During the hours that he should have been in the street, when contacted through the radio-talk, he couldn't be located. He was spending his time with female passengers, or just hanging out with other drivers at gas stations instead of working.

When Joe tried to warn him about his behavior for his own good, Afolabi became annoyed.

Afolabi had so many friends that the telephone never stopped ringing; this was causing great displeasure to his wife Carol.

Joe didn't want to risk another divorce, so he tried to straighten things out with Afolabi. However, Afolabi was listening more to his friends on the outside than he was to Joe.

Afolabi had even become vulnerable to arrest, for his documents had expired. He could be deported if apprehended by the Immigration authorities.

Joe advised him to work hard, save money, and get married for the 'Green Card', but he paid little attention to him. He still had it in his mind that he might be able to find Beatrice, marry her legally, and get it for free. In the meantime, he continued to go with many women.

Afolabi's sudden change from "Mr. Nice Guy" to a "louse" surpised Joe and Carol. For those who didn't want him to succeed, it was a time for rejoicing. As for Afolabi, it was a time for new alliances.

One day after Joe had gone to work, and Carol had taken the kids to school, Afolabi quickly and quietly moved out. He didn't even leave a good-bye note to inform them of his whereabouts.

Kofi Randy had come to America long ago. He was sent by his father's church to pursue theological study so he could return to serve the church. However, on his arrival in America, he refused to study. Instead he picked up a job at a service station.

Afolabi and Kofi became close friends. The car given to him as a gift had become a vehicle in which girls of various shapes, sizes and races were conveyed from party to party. This friendship had even made him forget about the search for Beatrice.

Nude parties with plenty of women and "booze" were frequently held in their spacious, gorgeous apartment overlooking the East River.

They hadn't the slightest idea they were both being driven by the devil slowly into a world of suffering, a world of hopelessness. Underlining the seriousness of their behavior was the background both came from in Africa-- a Christian home, a home in which one's elders were respected. But they felt they were in another land where these values were no longer important. They were totally deceived by their own ignorance and slowly being driven into the abysmal depths of oblivion. These few years in America had transformed Afolabi totally from a compassionate human being to a mindless 'good-timer" without direction or purpose. Kofi had been able to support his lifestyle from the money his parents continued to send him for the education they thought he was getting. He kept deceiving his parents about this education by taking picture of himself on various campuses and in libraries and mailing them home.

After Kudjo got back from Africa, where he had been studying his ancestral culture, he was surprised at the change in Afolabi. He knew his friend would suffer unless he learned another way.

Afolabi, for his part, saw no reason for such an abrupt change. He saw himself as a liberated man. He could do the things he wished to do. After all, that was what America was for. Everybody had the right to decide for himself whether to be somebody or nobody.

But he did forget one thing—he had no legal papers to remain in the country. He could be deported at any moment, if apprehended.

Meanwhile, Kofi's parent had grown tire of waiting for his return and stopped sending him money. He couldn't support his lifestyle any more. He became annoyed and stopped writing to his parents. The only letter he received from them subsequently was to inform him of his father's death. There was also a final appeal from the church leaders for him to return to head the church. He didn't pay them any mind. He and

A BURNING DESIRE

Afolabi continued to waste their youthful energies on frivolities. Their numerous tapes and records were their only source of pride, besides the thousands of pictures they had taken at parties, beaches, and nude dancers. They were happy they had "seen some life" at least once, but as their income diminished, they realized they would be seeing less and less of it.

They could no longer afford their fine "pad" and had to move out. The parties stopped and girls were now few and far between.

Kofi had his 'Green Card' but Afolabi did not. Kofi could collect unemployment checks but Afolabi could not.

Now even the car that had brought them so much pleasure became a bone of contention. Spare parts had become too expensive and one night when Kofi borrowed the car to go to a new girl friend's house, it was stolen. This brought misunderstanding between them. Afolabi was much stronger physically and threatened to beat Kofi. Kofi said he would report him to Immigration if he laid his hands on him.

Afolabi, now distrustful of Kofi and fearing he was no longer a friend, moved out. For the first time, he was on his own in America, without money or job. He knew he couldn't return to Joe.

Luckily, he was able to find a job in New Jersey. He realized he would have to adjust quickly to this new life, so he rented a cheap room in a delapidated hotel full of welfare recipients.

A BURNING DESIRE

Chapter XII

Meanwhile, the campaign against "illegal aliens" continued. Senators and congressmen attacked them. They were to be deported. The news media reported the arrests, the raids on factories and residences. Many citizens spoke out against the harsh treatment of the aliens. "America is a nation of immigrants," they said. Soon there was talk of granting amnesty to those living continuously in the country for a number of years, but Afolabi's study of the stated qualifications made him realize he was not eligible. This fact began to depress him. He tried not to think about it but the fear was always there.

He now understood how stupid and fooolish he had been to leave Joe's house. He had never suffered any hardship when he was with Joe.

His off-and-on smoking and drinking habit caught up with him and he now smoked and drank more than he had in Africa. His only major gain was the availability of food. He ate, smoked, and drank very well.

Afolabi was physically capable of working hard, but lacked the will to do so. He became indolent and bored on the job, getting to work very late and sometimes taking off without permission. With these bad work habits, he wound up changing jobs rather often. As an illegal immigrant, he would have been better off staying on one job and gaining some foothold for future eventualities.

The American dream had failed to materialize for him. The America he dreamed of and talked unceasingly

93

about in Africa had eluded him. He started to regret being in America.

But he could not return to Africa. He did not even have the plane fare. Plus he knew the even greater hardships that awaited him if he returned to the motherland. The worst he had been through in America was still mild compared with even his everyday life there.

The problems of responsibility had been mounting on him. He began to think of the ranch his father had promised to build him.

He had turned a deaf ear to the advice of many friends who had urged him to go to school or get married for the 'Green Card'. He had nobody to blame but himself. He could be sent back home empty-handed at any time. His hopes continued to diminish. Prospects became bleaker and bleaker every day. The search for Beatrice had proved fruitless. Since arriving he had never heard anything about her.

The marriage to America had been performed. The honeymoon was now over. He was quarreling with his bride. Divorce seemed imminent, reconciliation unlikely. She had lost all her glamour. This was not the love he had longed for and dreamed about for so many years. Now she bored him.

But one thing did not bore him: the reports that came in daily from the mass media telling of the arrest and deportation of millions of aliens. These reports frightened him so much they made his heart race. In fact, his heart raced so constantly he thought he might be suffering hypertension. But he would not go to a hospital for fear of being detected.

A BURNING DESIRE

He was displeased with the hassles of life in the United States. Whenever he looked around him, what did he see? Nothing that would energize him.

He watched with disgust how the older workers seemed to be addicted to work. All of them came in early and punched the time card. But he would always be late, although he could least afford the reduced earnings and the boss' displeasure. He was warned constantly about his lateness.

He studied these punctual workers closely and saw that they were indeed tired, but it was discipline that enabled them to hold on.

Afolabi looked around until he found some workers who acted and thought as he did. These became his new companions. After work they would get together and collect for a bottle of liquor. They drank in circles and smoked in chains. While some wrapped marijuana, others would light it. Their whole conversation consisted of complaints about the job and the people who supervised them

"He don't know me. I'm gonna blow his head off one of these days," said one of the men who was very annoyed with the boss.

"He asked me to sweep the damn floor," said another worker. 'I ain't come to sleep the floor,' I tol'm. 'If you ain't got no job, send me home.!"

"Bobby don't know me. I'm gonna beat the hit out of him. You wash tomorrow what I'm gone do to him," volunteered yet another concerning a foreman. They went on voicing their displeasure as they "got high" on liquor and marijuana.

This time Afolabi was just a listener. He didn't want to talk. His American slang was not that good yet. All he could do was be an active nodder to their statements and feelings.

A Jehovah's Witness working on the same job saw Afolabi's condition and advised him to cut off his bad habits. He told him that he himself had been saved by Jesus Christ, for he used to do the same things. But Jesus had made him a better person. Afolabi didn't listen.

But neither was the Jehovah's Witness happy about the job he was doing. He drew consolation from the thought of Christ's Second Coming. His faith kept him working unperturbed. He seemed to be in much better shape than those who were finding consolation in the bottle and in "grass." He sometimes characterized his position in the factory as "No future, presently." But he believed very faithfully that the Messiah would come to alleviate his suffering. When and how the Messiah was coming he couldn't tell.

With bills and other necessities of life to be met, Afolabi although not interested in working any more continued to work.

One day the Transport Workers Union issued a stike threat. Negotiations had been going on for weeks. The authorities worked very hard to prevent the strike but failed.

Car pools were set up for all city workers. Many companies rented cars for their employees. A new excitement was in the air. An inconvenience it was but it was also a welcome change from the routine monotony of subway and bus riding and the rigidity of the nine to five schedules. Lateness was no longer intolerable. New working hours were set up. Come early, go home early.

Television and radio stations were providing information as to what was to be done to deal with the crisis. The public was urged to "stay tuned" for major developments.

The night before the strike began, a boxing spectacular featuring the champions following Muhammad Ali was televised. Many New Yorkers went to bed late that night, especially the sports enthusiasts, hoping by the time they woke up everything would be settled.

Afolabi, being a sports fan, spent the night watching the fights. He went to bed about one in the morning to the sound of the strike announcement. He set his alarm clock for four and when the alarm sounded, he dashed out of bed and tuned in the radio for more strike details.

"The New York mass transit strike is on," said the announcer. Stay tuned for further developments." It was said it would probably be a very long strike due to the exorbitant demands of the workers. The city was not in a financial position to meet these demands. Soon the mayor was on the air asking New Yorkers to show courage and win the strike war. He encouraged them to beat the transit workers by formming car pools to get to work.

Afolabi happened to live in the same neighborhood as his co-workers. They were allocated the car that belonged to the company president's wife. It was a new

Ford station wagon, light blue in color with room for up to eight people. Most other workers had their own cars. Since he was the first to hear the news, Afolabi called the driver. The phone rang and rang but no one answered. The driver had watched the boxing that night with "the boys" and a half-gallon of Smirnoff vodka.

Afolabi waited a while and called again. Finally someone picked up the receiver.

"Hello," said a drunken voice. What's the story?" It was Jeff, one of the crowd he "hung out" with.

"Well, the strike's on" Afolabi told him.

"What? The strike's on?" he asked, somewhat sobered by the news. "Okay, get dressed and meet me in front of your house," he told Afolabi.

"I got dressed an hour ago," Afolabi replied.

"You didn't sleep?"

"I slept but got up early to hear the news."

"Okay, meet me there in about two hours," the driver said.

In two hours time, Jeff was at his door, his car filled with workers.

The car was also filled with marijuana smoke. "The weed" was being passed from hand to hand. Some more were being wrapped.

Jeff had his head shaved to the skin. No vestige of hair could be found on his head. He wore a T-shirt emblazoned with "Best World Paper Is Bambuu."

They started the ride from 130th Street on Broadway across the Triborough Bride to Queens, where they worked.

The smoke filled the car so much that Afolabi

decided to open the window on his side to let fresh air come in, only to face stiff objections from his co-workers. They did not want the smoke to get out. They wanted to inhale as much of the smoke as possible.

"This stuff is expensive and you don't wanna lose money, right?" said one of them.

Soon they were all coughing. Smells of yesterday's alcohol, mixing with marijuana engulfed the car. Afolabi defiantly opened the car window. This time there were no objections.

Every intersection was just so busy. A new zeal and verve had gripped the town.

The mayor himself was in the street congratulating and encouraging the people of the city. Many New Yorkers were caught unprepared. They didn't believe the negotiations would fail. They believed in the New York magic. But they were greatly disappointed.

Afolabi and his co-workers had great moments since they now had the freedom to ride, drinking and smoking, to and from work. During the strike, many people as well as cars thronged the streets. For the first time in the history of the city, hordes of human and vehicular traffic seemed almost equal in all the streets of this busy city. The bridges were all full of people moving to and fro. For many it was an adventure. For others it was a time to exercise, to get in tip-top shape--the New York shape (sexy-looking and healthy). Some roller-skated down the busy street, snaking past traffic jams with great skill, enjoying the music from their walk-a-matics. It was a great time for some cheats--the taxi drivers--to extract exhorbitant fares from the passengers by refusing to use their meters.

Just as the strike ended, Afolabi met an African woman named Ama. (He had given up on Beatrice.) Within a short time, they began living together. His new companion persuaded Afolabi to stop smoking and drinking, but a few weeks after they began their new life together, he lost his job.

Getting another job was very difficult. He couldn't go to the agencies to look for a job any more. The Immigration authorities were rumored to be rounding up aliens from the agencies as well.

Due to a lack of communication between him and his father, he had not immediately been informed of Kwame's death. It was only two years after his death that they sent him a letter through Kudjo with the news.

Afolabi mourned the loss of his father. He also worried about his property, for he knew it would be mismanaged. However, he had no immediate plans to go home. He was more concerned with his new love than with animals or land. He had a responsibility here, now.

Both the new tragedy at home and the new happiness he had found in America with his common-law wife made him sober up to his responsibilities. He began to consider the serious issues that faced him. He thought about the Jehovah's Witness' advice to accept Jesus Christ into his life. He thought of getting the Green Card, now that he had a woman in his life. But unfortunately, Ama was an illegal alien like himself. (She had entered the country on a now-expired student visa.) Now Afolabi had more than one problem to face. If both of them should get in trouble with Immigration at the same time, the results would be unthinkable. To avoid this, he decided to arrange a "Green Card marriage." He contacted some friends who knew Americans who married illegal aliens (on paper) so they could secure their status. Their marriageability was not entirely altrustic--it was in fact a paid service.

The contract brought very quick results. He married an Afro-American woman named Dorothy in two weeks. (Of course the marriage was not to be cosummated.) The woman understood her role very well and promised her full cooperation to enable Afolabi to become a legal resident.

Dorothy began to visit the couple often and have dinner with them. She especially enjoyed West African foods like 'fufu' and 'tebba' and the stews and soups that went with them. Whenever she visited them and Ama wanted to serve her American food, she objected and called for her African soul food ("Ancestors' food" she called it.)

The residence permit still had not arrived as of the time she demanded her payment ($1,500).

One cold wintry evening, Afolabi's door bell rang while he was fast asleep with his wife. The bell continued to ring until he awoke. He ran to the door and looked through the peep-hole. There was a woman standing there with all her belongings.

"What do you want?" he asked.

"Don't you recognize me?" Dorothy replied.

"Oh, I'm still sleepy. When I saw you with those

bags, I thought it was a stranger who had lost her way," he explained.

"Well, I've lost my apartment and I wanted to ask you if I could stay with you and your wife till I find another place."

"Okay, I'm coming," he said but instead he ran to Ama.

"Wake up, wake up and don't panic."

Ama woke and sat on the bed.

"Dorothy is pulling some kind of trick."

"What does she want?"

"She brought all her belongings with her and wants to stay with us awhile."

"All her belongings to stay with us for a a-w-h-i-l-e. H-u-u-m. She's coming to throw me out. She's coming to take over this place because she's on paper as your wife," said Ama, quickly discerning Dorothy's intentions.

"So let's refuse her then," Afolabi replied.

"But what if it's true she has nowhere to stay? And she is going to help you acquire the Green Card." An impulse toward compassion made Ama reverse her initially corect judgment.

So Dorothy was allowed into their house. Months passed and she made no attempt to move out. She wasn't even looking for a place. She had become a burden as well as a cause for arguments between Afolabi and Ama. She was making their marriage very difficult.

Finally when Afolabi looked for a place for her himself and tried to persuade her to take it, she boldly told him that Ama should move out instead. She had taken Ama's place by force.

Afolabi was flabbergasted and scared. He tried to put everything in order quickly before it got leaked out to the immigration authorities. He quickly arranged for Ama to move out. Afolabi hadn't planned to have two wives. But circumstances had forced it on him.

Ama, understandably, began to have doubts about the situation. She began to wonder if the whole thing hadn't been a plot between Afolabi and Dorothy to begin with. However, she couldn't pin-point any controversy that could make him do such a thing. They had had a beautiful, harmonious marriage.

The problem lay, quite obviously, with Dorothy. She had lost her boy friend to an African woman. Therefore, she was making Ama pay for something someone else had done. She had also lost her welfare benefits. She was told she was fit to work. These two things had driven her to take another woman's companion.

Afolabi commuted between his two women, although Dorothy enjoyed more of his presence than Ama.

Ama became very depressed and worried. She started to think about dissolving her relationship with Afolabi but Afolabi kept on telling her that she was still the wife of choice. He loved her, but the need to procure the card had made this unfortunate thing occur.

"You'll benefit from this at the end. Be a little patient," he continued to tell her. "Nothing is happening between us in the house. She's not sleeping in your bed. She sleeps on the couch," he told her truthfully.

A BURNING DESIRE

"I can't believe it! I can't believe it! Something is transpiring between you two in that bedroom," she cried jealously.

"Nothing is happening," he insisted.

Meanwhile, Afolabi was informed by his lawyers that it wasn't possible for him to get the Green Card through Dorothy anymore. Her records showed that she had used the same name to marry someone else. Knowing that they would be looking for her, she moved out.

On hearing this, Afolabi knew he had to move out too. Taking their most important things, he rushed to Ama's house where more electrifying bad news awaited him. Ama met him at the door with these words: "I'm sorry to tell you this. I hope you'll take it as a man. I don't love you anymore. I'm pregnant by a lover next door. Please continue your journey. I'll do you one favor and that is you can leave your bags with me and come for them another time."

Afolabi was shocked speechless. But Ama was right. No woman could take what happened--another woman coming into her house to throw her out. None could blame her for her actions. Furthermore, her new lover had promised to get her the Green Card because he was an Afro-American, a citizen.

"In situations of this nature, one needs a second man inside of him to help him fight the battle," Afolabi assured himself as he dashed to a liquor shop to buy a pint of whiskey. As he downed it, he surely felt like two. "I'll win someday," he assured himself again. "Women might fail me but one woman, my Mother Africa, will never fail me."

Chapter XIII

"Oh, Mother Africa, don't let me down. Oh, Mother Africa, don't let me down," he sang as he zigzagged his way towards his former hotel.

Glancing through the hotel directory board to see who had occupied his room, he came across two familiar names. These were the two Nigerians he met on the flight from Africa to America. They were doing all right but chose to live frugally.

The desk clerk phoned their room for Afolabi and they said it was all right to send him up. He ran upstairs, knocked on the door and announced himself.

"It's me, Afolabi. Oh, Mother Africa, don't let me down, don't let me down," he sang as he waited for the door to open.

"Your Mother Africa will never let you down. You have your brothers here--come on in."

"You're the one who came here from Africa with us some years ago? And you're still not settled yet?" one queried.

"America is not for me," Afolabi answered. "It's not for me," he repeated.

"If America is not for you then where in this world would be for you? The thing is, if you don't use your mind, you can't stay anywhere and be somebody," said one of his friends to him.

"I lost my wife and failed to get the Green Card," he told them.

"Wife and Green Card failed and you think the world is falling down on you? You don't know what happened to us when we first came here. You won't believe we slept in the Brooklyn Navy Yard because we didn't have the Green Card. And when we finally got it, what happened? Jobs couldn't be found. I had my degree and the green Card in my hands yet I couldn't find a job.

"I was advised by a friend to watch a T.V. evangelist whose message, he said, was so powerful that even if you were on your death bed, it would give you energy to walk again. If you've been looking for a job all your life and listen to him preach the Word of God to you, you'll get a job. I'd advise you to listen to him on Sunday. All your problems will end as soon as you start watching him and listening to him," his friend advised him. Look, we are now respected businessmen in West Africa. It's a waste of time to finish school and be here."

Afolabi had been hearing the message about God and His Son, but he never paid it any heed.

When he arrived in America he was very intelligent and knowledgeable, but his association with Kofi Randy had made him stupid.

His friends had gone into a beautiful partnership in Africa. They had bought some incubators, taken them home, and started their own poultry farms. Jobs had been provided to many of their brothers and sisters who might have been seeking avenues to come to America as well.

Afolabi was lucky. When they were going back to Africa, they paid his hotel bill for some few weeks to help him along. Even though they could have paid many years for him, they did not care to encourage him to be lazy. They figured if he had been serious about life in America, he would have elevated himself by this time.

Losing his wife and not being able to get the Green Card continued to depress him for some time, but as the days changed into weeks and the weeks into months, his depression lifted. He began to regain his self-confidence.

One night, he dreamt he was combing his hair. When he got up and looked in the mirror, he discovered that his hair had all turned grey.

From that day on, Afolabi knew the time had come for seriousness about life. Agressively, he started to pursue his earlier dreams--the dreams that brought him to America to become somebody and to change the ignorance of some of his people on the continent.

To enable him to get the things he needed, he took the suggestion of his African friends and started watching the television evangelist. Sometimes, if he felt bored, he went to church to meet some of his countrymen.

One day at church he heard it announced that contributions were being solicited for the Africans who were being expelled from Nigeria. Immediately Afolabi knew that his countrymen were among them. He had heard about it on the way to America, so it wasn't a surprise to him. He was sorry for his brothers and sisters, but what could he do? Nothing. Even though the expulsion order was criticized by many people throughout the world, including Americans, America was also arresting and expelling aliens. This annoyed Afolabi very much.

As the stories appeared in the news media, he knew

for sure that the Western press was only interested in sensationalism for the sake of increasing its readership.

"They were criticizing Nigeria, sacrificing her on the devil's altar when they created these situations themselves. They were publishing divisive statements that would pit one African nation against another. Who gave Africa all these boundaries? Who gave Africa all this miseducation? Who trained the law enforcement officers? Weren't they trained to be unsympathetic to their own race during the colonial period? Weren't the institutions of Africa made to be Western rather than African in orientation? Where is the African humanity that gave shelter to those lost at sea at Cape Horn--the same Europeans who became a thorn in Africa's flesh? Where are the materials that are miseducating my brothers and sisters to become consumers and not producers coming from? We are the victims of this miseducation. I must help African governments to adequately train their youths to love themselves," he said to himself on his way home.

One day after church again some of his countrymen brought up the plight of their brothers and sisters for discussion and possible remedy. Many of them were very annoyed with the government of Nigeria.

"You mustn't blame the government for doing that. Our government did the same thing not too long ago. I think some of you are too young to remember," said one of Afolabi's compatriots. This is a disaster for Africa, but we mustn't lose hope."

"What did they go there to do anyway? They should

have been working on the farms" said another.

"What farms?" someone asked.

"Don't tell me there are no farms in Ghana. I have brothers in Ghana as well. When my father died, I heard they sold some of the cows and went to Nigeria. They should have been working on the farm. Look, everybody is complaining we don't have this, we don't have that. Everything used by man comes from the land. We've all made a mistake by leaving our places of origin and settling abroad. We've got to return and do the things that will give direction to our brothers and sisters. But blaming Nigeria or the U.S.A. for sending illegal aliens away will not help us," Afolabi said.

"Have you been reading the papers or watching the television to see how they're being treated? one angry Ghanaian asked.

Afolabi answered, "Let's try to help them. There's no need crying over spilled milk. This is where we have a role in the total education of African people. Rules must be obeyed. Even in our country if you disobey the rules they treat you like animals. Why go into someone else's country without the qualifying papers? We're all to be blamed.

"The African police who treated their brothers and sisters so wickedly were simply ignorant. If they only realized that we are all Africans whether Nigerian, Malian, or Sudanese, they wouldn't have treated them so. They would have known that we are all one, coming from the same African roots all the way down to the Nile Valley. Alkebu-lan (one of the ancient names of

Africa) originally had no boundaries. We used to travel freely across the continent under the command of our kings and queens. Today white men have divided us, sliced us and cut us into pieces giving us regional names, drawing imaginary lines across our very own continent. They have succeeded in giving us weapons to fight each other. The artificial boundaries weren't created by God, but by men. Therefore, with clear understanding, with the same intentions, with the same knowledge of our Africanness, born out of the same fathers and mothers many years back, we could surmount many of the obstacles placed on our forward movement as African people. For today we may be regionally divided and named. Tomorrow through future generations we shall not be this nation or that but forever and ever Africans shall we be within the continent or without the continent," for one mustn't think that his or her generations shall forever be this national or that national, this tribe or that tribe. There's no racial or tribal purity. We are all but mixed people, one people. If today you're a Fulani tomorrow your children's children may be an African-American not a Fulani. Therefore only African shall we and our generations be forever and not this national or that national or this tribe or that tribe. It's time we develop "maturedly" with a higher level of knowledge to live above less important things like tribalism and so called nationalism. For if all our ancestors were to come out today, we may see them as of different tribes to what we are today. What mattered most is our African identify - same African people living on this earth - This would solve our problems today continentwide," he concluded.

"You said it all," they exclaimed.

"I hope people like you will return to start doing something to bring direction to the continent's people," said another, encouraging Afolabi to continue to speak out.

"Africa's problem is no problem. It could be solved. We've got to be industrious, creative and productive for ourselves. Look, farming could be done on a very large scale, giving jobs to millions, from those working in the fields to those harvesting, down to the beautiful African ladies who would be selling the food in restaurants. Millions of youths could be employed.

Instead of relying on imported items from needles to pens and paper, indigenous Africans could develop new technologies to suit our markets, so that things that are being imported now could be produced on the continent. By these means, jobs could be available for all Africa's young people.

This is the reason we became independent. Our independence, African independence, is meaningless unless the African mind is set free to dream, to meet the needs of the people, and to create and develop the resources of our motherland.

Unless the African mind is able to bring waters to the dry lands of Africa, unless the African mind is able to discover that there is a reason behind God's creation of land and rivers and oceans, then we will always die by the thousands whenever there is drought.

111

A BURNING DESIRE

In every nation on earth there is a river large enough to be utilized for survival when it does not rain. Why, then, should the children of Africa, the mothers of Africa be suffering and yearning for rain to fall to water their crops? It's only by the liberation of the African mind that the deserts will bloom.

The people in the Northern deserts were able to transform these into forests by bringing icebergs from the Polar regions to water the crops.
They planted crops and trees to make life livable in these once deserted territories.

It's only the African mind that can fill the hospitals with drugs for our sick children, mothers and aged fathers. It's only the African mind that can produce the same things made in the white man's land that are shipped to us to be consumed by the ton while creating jobs for their people.

"It is only by hard work that we survive wherever we are. How foolish we are to be chasing 'the good life' from one end of the earth to the other when we could be creating it for ourselves right where we are. If others can change our deserts into forests, we can change our forests into farming lands, orange orchards, pineapple plantations and industries and factories for pulp and paper, food, clothing, cars—whatever we need or want. We can then have Ibadan Fried Chicken, Lagos Fried Chicken, Entebbe Fried Chicken, Accra Fried Chicken, Enugu Fried Chicken, Harare Fried Chicken and Dakar Fried Chicken to feed all hungry mouths on the continent.

"Such a program of comprehensive agricultural and

A BURNING DESIRE

industrial development would beautify the motherland that has held us throughout the centuries." He spoke as if possessed by an intense force that came from the very heart of Africa itself. What he said, his compatriots could identify with. They all left the church that day speechless.

In a minuscule but significant way, Afolabi had begun his duty to his motherland and her people. He had begun to understand the hard truth about the world. He had been to the factories and in the streets. Now he had to settle down and study carefully how America had been developed and how Africa could be developed the same way.

By begging his Mother Africa never to forget him or let him down, he had humbled himself. He had become a new person.

One day he thought, "Mother Africa knows that too often those who could do something about the plight of the continent, on account of selfish material considerations and interests, choose not to do anything."

"It's surprising to see African doctors, trained with the poor African taxpayers' money running away from them to work overseas where they aren't needed, because they claim a lot of equipment required for their work isn't available. Therefore, they won't stay and work on the continent to save their sick and suffering people.

"Where can this equipment be found? Who is going to develop it for them? Why don't they sit down and figure out a way to produce the equipment themselves?

113

With this new vision, a superabundance of goods and services would always be there, flowing unceasingly like the waters of the Nile, like the waters of the Volta and like the waters of the Niger into the needy homes, factories, and hospitals of Africa. This way African life would not be a life of suffering, misery and lamentation."

A BURNING DESIRE

Chapter XIV

Beatrice, Afolabi's first girl friend, had married very soon after arriving in the United States. She now had a ten-year-old boy. (Of course, Afolabi knew nothing of this). Her husband was on scholarship from Africa. However, when the government that sponsored him was overthrown, he lost his scholarship. He worked very hard to support himself through college, with Beatrice' help. Unfortuntely, he couldn't find any job in the United States, so they moved to Canada where he got a job as a computer analyst.

Beatrice' husband (John Tutu by name) for all this, lacked any real affection for his wife. For some reason, she could not conceive by him and he wanted children. This circumstance led him to neglect her, throwing himself into his work instead. Beatrice as a young woman needed love, but she couldn't get it from her husband.

Since John was only the third man she had known, her mind naturally returned to her first lover, Afolabi, for a woman never forgets her first lover. (Her second lover, the German engineer, no longer had any place in her thoughts or feelings).

Beatrice did not even know how to get in touch with Afolabi. She had tried six years earlier to bring him from Africa so they could marry, but the person she had sent came back claiming he had found out that Afolabi had been arrested for stealing and was jailed for life.

Beatrice didn't believe Afolabi would do such a

thing. He and his aunt were God-fearing and they had enough money to live decently. She believed the man was lying, because as soon as he delivered his message, he tried to buy her favors with money but she refused him.

Unable to get any satisfaction from her husband, Beatrice became very unhappy and started agitating at home.

"I'm a young woman. I need love. You can't love your job more than me. How many times do I see you in a week? You don't know what day my birthday is. You don't know whether my parents are alive or dead. Look at the letters arriving from home. Food is very expensive back home. I worked hard to look after you in college. And now that you have your degrees and are working and making all that money, you don't even know me. You satisfy your parents and brothers and sisters back home in Africa, but not me whom you sleep with. I give you allthe love I have in me, yet you treat me and my poor son like non-persons.

"I know this child is not yours, but one day he'll certainly find his father, and his father will give him all the love he needs. Not a single day since we've been together have you arrived home from work with a toy for this son. Is that how people treat their family? You think that only your mother, brothers and sisters are your family. But as for me and my poor boy, we're nothing but dirt in your eyes.

"But when night comes you know how to sleep with me and satisfy yourself. That's all you do -- satisfy yourself!

A BURNING DESIRE

"If you don't do something about this you'll be crying for my love. I'm a good woman. I do everything for you. That's the way my mother taught me before I left home for this country. And that's how I'll always be. If I leave you, you'll be sorry," she said, crying to her husband as they slept together for the last time.

The next morning, after her husband went to work thinking of what she had told him the night before, Beatrice packed her belongings and left for New York.

"I need love like any other woman," she said upon arriving in New York City. "How can you love a nation without knowing how to love just the two people in your own house? How can you be a president without putting your own house in order? Or does one become a president just to steal the nation's money and deposit it in foreign bank accounts? These were her reflections on her husband's behavior and attitudes for it seemed Mr. Tutu wanted to become a president. In fact, that and his job were all he thought about. The only thing he bragged about was the degrees he thought qualified him to become the president of an African republic.

But she had had enough both of his ambitions and his cruelty. In the past when she said something John didn't like, she found her luggage flying through the air and her clothing about to be set ablaze. Then she would beg for forgiveness.

Now she was in New York, having finally found the courage to make her break. Perhaps she might be lucky enough to find a lover who would fulfill her desires as a woman.

A BURNING DESIRE

Afolabi stood in violation of the law and was therefore very cautious. He had no right to be working when his visa had expired, and he had filed fraudulent papers to obtain a residence permit. He would be deported immediately if detected.

If he should ever be sent home, he would be more miserable than he had ever been. More aliens had arrived in his country, and the situation there wasn't easy at all. Although international agencies had airlifted some relief supplies, they weren't enough. The nation's past neglect of farming had aggravated the situation. As parents got old and unproductive, and children who could handle only paper and pen weren't willing to replace them in the traditional livelihood of agriculture, food production decreased. For Afolabi, to be sent home to meet these hardships would be worse than life imprisonment.

As he learned more about the troubles brewing in Africa, he decided to work even harder. He began to save money after picking up two jobs. In a few months time, he saved more money than he had ever saved since arriving in America--a feat achieved through thrift. Now that he felt somewhat secure financially, he looked for a woman to marry.

Just as the criticism of Nigeria's expulsion of aliens ended in the American press, the immigration officers mounted a large round-up of illegal aliens unlike anything in U.S. history. From factory to factory they went, with or without warrant, arresting aliens. Terror gripped the alien community.

It was the end of a difficult campaign, and it was

rumored that a conservative candidate would win the election. Therefore, the new immigration officers were "cleaning house" before he took office.

Many aliens were arrested in the two-week sweep. Just as aliens were being rounded up, Afolabi, coincidentally, began to experience serious difficulties on the job. Since he was reliable and worked hard, he was very quickly promoted by his new boss. This displeased his former boss, a racist second-generation Italian-American, who hated Afolabi for his color alone.

Despite his antipathy to Afolabi, however, he had no grounds to dismiss him, so he transferred him to the dirtiest job in the factory.

Afolabi understood his situation only too well. He knew that he had no residence papers, no "Uncle Sam," and no relatives in America, and the only way he would keep a roof over his head and pay his bills was to do whatever he had to bring in the money. So he accepted the mean job and did it with distinction.

Upon seeing how well he did his job, the new boss in that department made him a shipping and receiving clerk.

Within two days, Afolabi had a desk with telephones. He could sit down anytime he wanted to. Afolabi had become the highest-ranking black on the job. His duties called for him to work with the white men and women in the main office. This they resented very much. To try to hurt his reputation, they (especially a female office worker) began to report him unfavorably to the president of the company.

He was falsely accused of stubbornness, rudeness,

and spending too much time on the telephone. For all that, Afolabi was less worried about being fired than he was about someone dropping a dime on him. Through it all, his immediate boss, a Jew, stuck with him, even telling him secretly that he saw talent in him.

As his difficulties on the job increased, he became very frustrated and annoyed with the position of Africa's leaders. "For" he said, "they have refused to make life livable back home in Africa."

Meanwhile, on the job, the union had stepped in to keep Afolabi from being fired, but this only increased the white opposition's resentment. The conservative mood that was sweeping America and threatening to sweep the illegal aliens away along with it disturbed him deeply. He felt as if he were going crazy. He became a human volcano, ready to erupt at any minute. But as he began to weigh and analyze things, it all started to come together.

Beatrice had found a place to live in New York City with her son. Because her son was born in America and was therefore a citizen, his mother qualified for a few benefits, since she wasn't working. Unfortunately, the conservative Republican candidate won the election. Poverty-stricken families were distressed, for the President had warned that all able-bodied persons would be stopped from receiving social benefits.

While those who thought they were safe were joyous over the election results, fear and uncertainty gripped the illegal alien community. Afolabi became very cold and feverish.

"This country was built with courage and people

willing to take chances, so I'll be very courageous,"
he told himself.

As he looked forward to meeting a woman to marry so
he could get his residence permit, he continued the
search for Beatrice. He knew he had made a mistake by
not looking for her during the first years of being in
the city.

He knew the new President would be carrying forward
one of his campaign promisses -- getting rid of
undesirable, undocumented aliens. Both the outgoing
President and the incoming President had publicly
deplored the action of the Nigerian government, so if
their criticism was anything other than bald hypocrisy,
why not give amnesty to America's aliens?

The answer, according to the President, was that
unemployment was so high that the arrest and
deportation of illegal aliens was necessary to give
Americans their jobs back.

As soon as he took the Oath of Office, new rules
were instituted. All able-bodied people had to go and
look for jobs. In some ways the President was right,
because with the availability of Aid to Dependent
Children, many women didn't respect their husbands
anymore. The welfare system had not united families.
It had rather encouraged them to split over small
disagreements, since support could easily come from big
"Uncle Sam." It seemed the role of the parents in the
family had been taken over by the government.

Drastic changes had occurred among people coming
from Africa as well. Many left their husbands knowing
very well that they qualified for help from the
government.

A BURNING DESIRE

Beatrice was struck from the welfare rolls. She had to go and look for a job. She had a child to support. She still wished she could meet his father. She wondered why for so long Afolabi didn't make any attempt to leave Africa to come to America. As she wondered, she concluded that Afolabi and others didn't need to come to the United States. (She had no idea he already had and was eagerly looking for her.)

"People like Afolabi shouldn't come to America," she thought. "They have money and there is no reason for them to be here. I wished I had known what life would be like here. I wouldn't have come either."

Many immigrants felt the same as Beatrice. Even though they had the residence permit, they still failed to achieve any goals in the United States.

One Saturday, as Afolabi was going to buy some shoes on 125th Street, he came across a black preacher. He was surrounded by many people, both black and white. One white man remarked to his wife, "Angels won't come in white anymore. This is the way they'll appear to us these days," he said as they made their way toward the speaker.

It was very unusual to see crowds of whites and blacks mixing in the streets of Harlem, listening to a gospel of the hidden truth about life.

The preacher seemed to have made most of his talk before Afolabi arrived on the scene. However, he heard enough to carry him on.

"The use of the mind for creation is the sole aim why God gives us the brain," said the man. "Every living thing, He created -- the ants, the bees, the trees."

A BURNING DESIRE

Hallelujah," echoed the crowd.

Some black Christian folks seemed to be spiritually possessed upon hearing the name of God or the Lord mentioned.

"The powers inherent in you and your brain if utilized properly can move mountains of suffering from your way. God is in you because everybody here is made in His image. And if the God in you is used to provide good things, you'll become happy. If you think of being rich and use the God in you properly, you'll become rich. But if you don't and you discourage yourself from doing it or using it, you'll forever be very poor and very unhappy, he said as the crows shouted, "Amen! Hallelujah! praise the Lord!"

The small crowd that had surrounded him earlier had increased tremendously. Some paid serious attention to what was being said while others just stood giggling. People of all shapes, all colors, people in shappby clothes, and some well-dressed, both old and young surrounded him. Some continued to push drugs on an adjacent street corner.

"How do you become rich? By using your brain to create a marketable commodity, skill or the end result -- goods that will bring comfort and pleasure to others," he said.

"You've got the magnet in you to bring good things to you and your family. Knowing also we're made of the earth, and knowing too that the earth we live on got magnet inside it. What are the things drawn by the magnet of the earth?

"All living things, humans, birds, trees, fishes.

They grow old because of the magnet in the earth attracting us to give way to others to live. It wears and tears us down so that more room could be created for generations to continue. You die fast if the God in you is not utilized to benefit you or others in order to withstand the force of attraction. You have that force -- that God in you to attract something to you."

This man was speaking as if he had been to school in another world. All the things he was saying, people could relate to. So the throng kept growing larger.

"Now I'm going to talk about prayer. You have to pray to God, because if you pray, you're energizing your soul, your spirit, your force within you. Not only that, you're also confiding in yourself, your God-given ideas," he said smiling.

"Hey, man. Do you want a place to do your preaching? Because all the things you're saying here are of greater significance than the things people go to church and listen to every Sunday all year round. This is why some of us dropped out of church. I want to live my life here on earth before I die and not when I die and I'm put in the grave. Most people going to church these days are helping in providing a better living for their pastors only, while they are being told to obey and follow the teachings of the Lord so that they can go to heaven when they die.

"I personally didn't see any truth in those philosophies, so that's why I stopped going to church. And if I should be good to my family and friends, I think I should be able to provide for their needs be they monetary or otherwise. After all, I'm alive, not dead and in the tomb. Does this make any sense? Or has it any relation to what you are telling us?" questioned a member of the audience at break time.

"You've got some points out there. However, you're wrong to say Pastors live off churchgoers luxuriously. That's the devils ideology. Pastors live on their God-given talents. They preach and teach the wisdom of God. They are the shepherds. Modern day drivers of God's people. Without them the journey through life would be more troublesome, more confused. Without Pastors, they'd be no churches. They'd be more than double the number of people on drugs, being killed by ignorance, frustration, confusion in our streets and homes. You name it! All the evils flooding the homes and sweeping people down the drain. The churches provide the way up to God - through Jesus."

"Look at the men and women running away from homes. They can't accept responsibility but do accept irresponsibility. I have come down the street today to preach because of you who are shunning the churches and being driven by evil to your doom. Go to church for Salvation ! Salvation ! Salvation ! I have a church come and get on the wagon of salvation with me. But be ready to pay your dues. Priase the Lord and rejoice for giving yourself to Him. Because of Him you can cross the mighty oceans of ignorance, climb formidable mountains of woes. No matter where you are, you need God whether in Africa, South America or Japan. Let Jesus Christ be your director and guardian. Call on His name and all the heavenly gates shall be open for you. Pray and your ideas would materialize."

Amen, Amen, Halelujah, Halelujah, the crowd shouted with fists and open palms into the air.

After resting for a few minutes the Pastor began talking again amidst the clapping of many hands. They wanted to hear more.

Afolabi was so exhilarated from the street lecture that he forgot he was going to buy shoes.

"Prayer is the food of the spirit, the force behind the many ideas we have in us. Music is the food of love, so play it," the preacher continued. "Pray to affirm the thoughts, the ideas within your mind. Pray to fertilize your ideas so they will grow and bear fruit. Prayer is the key that can open hidden spiritual doors. Why are millions traversing the globe from one end to the other? They lack the power of attraction. Many people are grumbling, 'they cut our social benefits'. No more welfare checks are coming in." Why should someone else give you the things you need?

"God knows why he created you black. He knows why you are born handicapped. He knows why He made you poor. Any misfortune you find yourself in is a challenge for you to overcome and be somebody.

"I'll end my message with a short story. A small island was inhabited by some people many years ago. They were all ignorant of the geological formation of their island. Another island a few miles away had knowledgeable people from second island quickly took over the first and found more oil there than they had on their own island.

126

A BURNING DESIRE

"Your mind can alleviate all kinds of suffering for you only if let it work for you. That's why God created us in His own image, giving us His power to do the things that will make us happy.

"Today a man or woman, a child or an old person is not legally dead unless........," he paused.

"He's completely brain dead," Afolabi filled in quickly.

"You got it, you got it, my son." He ended his preaching by praising Afolabi for his answer.

The crowd roared with laughter and applause as the meeting broke up. Everybody left with something from this black man to help him reach his personal goal in life.

As the talk ended, Afolabi was very happy he had met this man and had learned a lot that day from him. He was especially joyous over the correct answer he had been able to give.

A BURNING DESIRE

Chapter XV

As he headed towards the shoe store, which was only some few yards from the preaching site, he was confronted by some Negro youths who demanded all his money.

Afolabi protested but they were already on him, surrounding him. He was caught in the middle.

"You gave the man the answer to the question, right? We know you ain't from this country, right? You from somewhere in the jungle--Africa, right? When you going home to Zululand? Get out the money you got on you, nigger," he commanded.

"I'm your brother," said Afolabi.

"No, no, you ain't my brother--this is my brother." He twisted his fingers to show his brother. This tall heavy Negro doing the talking while his companions giggled and smiled, seemed to be the leader of the band.

"Give out that money or you'll have this in your balls," he said, pulling along knife from his pocket. It was sharp, too.

Afolabi obliged very quickly on seeing the knife. He gave them the fifty dollars he had on him. They left him after taking him down about half a block to camouflage their actions.

This incident sapped away Afolabi's joyous confidence in the preacher's words.

"Black people hurting black people. And the white man is to be blamed for this? Oh, I nearly died. Why do this to me? I've never been held up in New York.

This may be a sign for me to do something to get out,"
he said to himself on the way to the bank to withdraw
more money for his shoes.

When he was about a block away from his bank, he
saw a lot of people. Police cars were all around.
Security was very tight, with police lines preventing
unauthorized crossing. It seemed as if something very
serious was happening inside the bank. As he got
nearer, he could see movie cameras inside and out. The
police sirens and ambulance sirens were on. The
onlookers watching the scene inside clearly were really
having fun.

As Afolabi got a better view of the show inside, it
not only surprised but disgusted him as well.

"What happened to me a few minutes ago would have
been better for a movie," he angrily remarked.

There was a movie being made about a bank robbery.
And instead of using guns as robbers normally do, they
were using snakes and human skulls.

"This is a disgrace. This is where the copycats--
those guys in the street robbing people--get their
ideas," he said.

Those who had witnessed the showing earlier spoke
of how tellers, bank officials and customers had
fainted. Some of the elderly customers had even had
heart attacks and had to be rushed to the hospital.
But it was clear the spectators were enjoying it all.
They described how skulls were given to the tellers in
money bags.

The officers were kept at bay, frozen with fear at
the sight of crawling snakes. Their eyes were glazed

and their hands shivering. They just couldn't do anything. The snakes were crawling around inside the bank looking for an exit. As for the robbers, they were long gone.

They came in as well-dressed businessmen, their trunks loaded with those creatures to fool the bank officials.

Many predicted the movie would be a success.

"This is immoral in a sense. But in a sense too, it's certainly acceptable, when you consider the jobs and money it'll bring in," said two beautiful blonde onlookers.

"The bottom line is what people worry about these days, flat or uphill" said another, as they laughed it off.

Afolabi knew the movie would do well and people would enjoy it. The overall beneficiary would be the government. It would collect taxes on the film. Money would then be advanced towards the citizens' well-being. Jobs would be created, entertainment would be provided and it would be business as usual.

"Were these the ideas that the black man was talking about? Of course ideas made America great--ideas and people willing to take chances on them. Benjamin Franklin discovered electricity by taking a chance. The Wright Brothers took a chance and today airplanes are flying all over. Alexander Bell took a chance and developed the telephone. Today space is being explored by nations willing to take chances. This is the meaning of creativity--the use of the brain to dare the impossible and make life better for people," Afolabi thought. If Africa able to take these chances?

Afolabi had had a very rough day. Never before had he been through so many activities in one day. He therefore decided to postpone buying the shoes.

On his arrival home, he found, to his surprise, two letters from half-brothers in Africa. He quickly read the letters. The message inside was both dreadful and annoying: they were in dire straits and needed his money.

"This is no time to worry about them. I've got to achieve my own goals first and then they will be considered. How can I carry anyone now when I have no backbone?" he said after reading the letters.

He put the two letters away, picked out some books on philosophy and headed towards Riverside Park.

"Better for me to read some words of wisdom than those letters," he said to himself.

He found an empty seat under some trees; their shade made the area very cool that hot summery day.

"This is the poor man's air-conditioned den," he said, laughing at his own words.

He selected one of the books written by the t.v. evangelist and began reading his favorite chapter on "Possibility Thinking."

Just as he was getting involved in his reading, he heard the shuffling of feet through the fallen leaves on the ground.

He tried hard to ignore it, but no matter how he tried, the shuffling continued to disturb his concentration. He decided to stop reading until the person walked by. The man, who seem to be a little bit intoxicated, changed direction and started walking directly towards him. Afolabi quickly went into a defensive posture in case the approaching person were as vicious as the ones who had robbed him earlier.

Coincidentally, it was Kofi Randy, his friend from the good-time days. Afolabi's bitterness about their bad parting had faded with time and he rose to greet him.

"Randy," he yelled, subverting his intended goal suddenly.

"Afolabi, you're still alive? I thought you had died.
What are you doing here?"

"Reading."

"Some dirty books or what?"

"Dirty books! They belong to the past. No time for them now. I'm reading books of knowledge to redeem Africa."

"Redeem Africa? You got time to waste on Africa? Redeem me first. Give me some money. I'm broke. The welfare check got delayed. It should have arrived yesterday, but for some reason--"

"What? You're on welfare, Randy?"

"What's wrong with that?"

"Is that why you're here in America? You should be helping the brothers and sisters back home. But you're receiving welfare. How can you even support any of your family?"

"Family? Afolabi, are you on drugs? Who is supporting his family now? You mean in America or in Africa?

"Both places."

"You must be joking. With the cost of living so high, how can you support your children? I left them up to the government to support. I ran away from them. Their mother can find support from the relief agencies."

"I can't believe you're saying this. You who were sent here to return to be a leader have turned out to be an irresponsible person--not even responsible to your own children."

"I thought you had also changed like me. So it was a blessing when we broke up," Kofi retorted.

"Come on, forget about those days. Don't bring that up now," Afolabi pleaded. He continued in the same earnest tone, "We go through changes in life and you must chance with the times. Those days in America were acclimatizing days. There are important things facing us on the continent. Those days are over now. We've grown older. Grey hairs are appearing on our heads now. We've got to think not like children but like adults. Why do you demean yourself, your African self by depending on public assistance?"

"Are you jealous of me for being on welfare?"

"Huh, jealous? I hardly think so."

"Sure, who wants to be working in a factory these days?" Kofi demanded.

"Very soon you'll lose those benefits. You see how they are cutting people off? How can you pay your bills when you don't work? How can you buy the things you want so much? Let me tell you, if you're an able-bodied person and receiving welfare, it's like being buried alive slowly."

"Hey, when in Rome do as the Romans do," remarked Randy.

"And that means being on welfare, I suppose. Let me tell you, being on welfare is like being a brain-dead person. Something has to be done about you. You're telling me that even to buy underwear the government has to give you the money. There are opportunities here. Learn something to be self-supporting."

"You know how many people are receiving benefits? Not only me. A lot of people. Even friends from Africa are receiving benefits."

"So you follow the crowd."

"I ain't no fool. The thing is there. Why shy away from it?"

"I heard from an old buddy you were arrested by Immigration at one time. Is it true?" Randy said, trying to change the topic.

"If I had been, what would you and he have done to help get me out? That's what you folks from our motherland know. You know how to talk negatively about people. You won't sit down and use your precious time to learn something to benefit yourselves and mankind. You're always gossiping about this man and that woman. And most of the time the person you're wasting time discussing is making more progress than you because he's utilizing his time wisely. But just for the record, I never have been and never will be arrested."

"Give me some money," Kofi again demanded.

"So you're still with the bad habits?"

"Hey, how can you fight the pressures of the city,

which is even more than when we first arrived if you don't take anything to make you happy? I should have made some money already by ....." he paused. Randy slowly pulled out a long knife from under his jacket.

"What? You're sticking up people now? Please spare me. I just got robbed the same way."

"Don't yell. I'm only demonstrating to you how we make part-time money. I'm not gonna stick you up."

"But you scare me. You shouldn't have shown me that knife. I've seen one today already."

For protection's sake, Afolabi also had a knife with him.

"You see this is for my protection," Afolabi said, showing him his knife also.

"Yeah, everybody's getting armed. I'll have to stop carrying mine, said Randy.

"It's very risky for you, sticking up people to make a living," said Afolabi. "Tomorrow go to church and seek the Spirit of God to lift you up. You're sinking very fast." You've one more time to come up before finally sinking.

"When did you become like this?"

"Since leaving you."

"You believe in church. I bet you're one of the people helping the pastor to ride in those beautiful, luxurious cars."

"It doesn't matter, as long as we're getting some spiritual direction. I think it's better than sticking up people with knives and losing one's vision of how beautiful life can be." "Why don't you become a pastor so that people could help you live luxuriously?"

"You're wasting my time. I should have made some fast bucks for the day and gone to bed."

"Wasting you time? You had better do something now before you're wholly immersed in the hell of everlasting suffering. Yours is getting to be serious. You've discarded the God in you--the good in you--and filled yourself up with devilish thoughts. There are no good vibrations in your mind. You're not feeding your brain cells with positive, good thoughts--heavenly thoughts. Instead you're feeding you mind with negative thoughts and hellish intents. Because of this you're looking like a devil. If you plant cotton seed, you get cotton. You're planting inside your mind devilish seeds, poisonous plants, so you're getting bad results. Go to church and redeem yourself. Read these books and they will energize your brain cells and once again you can redeem yourself."

Had Afolabi's words worked on him? He kept silent.

"Now by reading these books not only have I learned the truth why some countries are greater and more prosperous than others, but also I've discovered the universal magic formular for life. Nobody will make you happy. Only you can make you happy.

"Nobody can make Africa a paradise except we Africans. Only knowledge about ourselves, who we are and where we come from can transform Africa into what we want it to be--what it should be. Only then will we see smiling faces on the children of Africa, on the mothers of Africa, and on all African people. Then there will be no more coups d'etat, no more suffering and no more yearning for this and that. That's the

only time when life in the four corners of Africa shall
forever and ever blossom. Then there shall be no more
criss-crossing of the earth in search of bread and
butter, milk and honey by both those who should know
better and those, like you and me, so ignorant that we
are sitting down here under this foliage hiding knives
under our jackets, slowly being buried alive by welfare
checks. Look at where we are. We who should be the
torchbearers of our African brothers and sisters are
being blinded by ignorance and miseducation. Isn't
that pathetic to our very own, mother Africa? We in
America must be the Symbol of Prosperity, Progress and
Procurement for mother Africa."

"Let's open up the gates of every frontier in
Africa. In so doing we Africans shall become free from
bondage to the outside world. This way African talents
can be free to operate, to discover and produce the
basic things we as Africans need. Why did we fight for
independence if we are going to keep going to the same
colonial enemies—whom we imagine to be our friends—to
buy our food, clothing, and shelter? And once we can't
pay them, we become international debtors, because we
have so little to sell, so little to dump on them. And
even the things we do have to sell, the price is
decided by them," a strong, productive, smiling Africa
would emerge only when we Africans can sue our minds to
dynamite the mountains of woes from the continent. And
instead of being security guards, chauffeurs and
hotel-keepers at night in foreign lands, we become the
bosses of the industries that grow out of our African
mind, living comfortably, providing decent jobs to

A BURNING DESIRE

African Youths; Afolabi concluded. He saw Kofi Randy as Africa going down the drain and spoke with a burning desire for Africa's redemption.

"You surprised me with the knowledge you have. Where and when did you become so enlightened? What's your telephone number?'

"I don't give my number to anybody. But because it's you I shall give it to you."

"I'll call you as soon as I get home."

"Okay, do that. And please, Randy, go to church. You'll be a better person for it."

"I'll think about it."

"And please go home straight. Don't go hunting."

With a smile and a hoarse laugh he left him.

"This is how I would have become if I hadn't left this man. Oh, mother Africa, I thank you."

"Oh I forget to introduce him to this church on 145th Street, Convent Avenue, for our African-American Professors to liberate his mind before it's too late", he soliloquized.

As he got up momentarily to see if he could catch a glimpse of him, it began thundering and lightening very fiercely that Afolabi had no option but to head home quickly. Soon afterwards, it started raining. The outdoor activities came to a sudden halt as the rain poured down ruthlessly forming streams by the curbsides.

Sitting down by his window, he watched closely the many people who were loosing their mass-produced umbrellas as they struggled in vain against the gusty winds.

New demands for umbrellas would lead to the

creation of more jobs. The tune for the cleaning of the streets would be led by the Sanitation Department. Jobs! jobs! jobs!

Afolabi's wandering mind came to many ideas which, when instituted, would change Africa into a "paradise". Western countries were made "so" because of many ideas. Dreams and ideas quickly turned into realities provided jobs. The presence of millions of roaches and rats in apartment houses had led to the creation of millions of jobs. The need for food had led to massive agricultural undertakings in the United States of America. Mental Power! Super Power!

"I look around me; jobs! jobs! jobs! Rain falls; jobs! Sunshines; jobs! When the land is dried; jobs! Desires for better looking, desires for happiness and glamor; for more knowledge about space; for more lasting live - longevity; desires for people to find salvation in the Great Almighty; desires to make modern homes become garden of flowers - jobs! Desires to praise the Lord our Savior in Hallelujah songs - jobs! Everything is job. But what about Africa?" he chuckled.

Nodding his head in disbelief and discontent and with eyes fixed on the letter from his exiled brother, tall and handsome Afolabi started yawning. Tiredness and too much worry in a single day took a toll on him. His head began to dance to the "rain music" - comforting natural music of relaxation. Afolabi fell into deep sleep.

Rain and sleep. A rejuvenation. A rebirth. Nature ought to be satisfied. "That's how life goes around, that's how life goes around," he snored.

A BURNING DESIRE

Chapter XVI

It had been three years since the Amnesty Bill had been in Congress. Each year the honorable representatives had debated it without result.

However, in the summer of 1985, both Houses of Congress gave up the filibustering and tentatively passed the Amnesty Bill. The President, who himself was very eager to have the bill passed, cut short his vacation in the Caribbean and signed it into law. With the signing of the bill, joy erupted like a volcano in the alien communities of America. It was as if a huge weight had been lifted from the aliens. Many people took to the streets to have a good time, to celebrate.

In no time, amnesty paraphernalia were being sold on the streets--buttons, T-shirts, and caps of all sizes. They bore such words as:

I"M A 100% LEGAL ALIEN

I"M NOW A CITIZEN

NO MORE ILLEGAL ALIENS IN THE USA

NO MORE IMMIGRATION OFFICERS

GREEN CARD FOR FREE

NO MORE GREEN CARD AGENTS

ALL IMMIGRATION OFFICERS HAVE LOST THEIR JOBS

NO MORE JOBS FOR FEDERAL PLAZA PEOPLE

SHOW ME THE WELFARE CHECK OFFICE

NO MORE SWEAT SHOPS

NO MORE DROPPING A DIME ON ME

I CAN GO HOME AND COME BACK WITHOUT FEAR

Afolabi was lucky. He had never been arrested since he had arrived in America, although he had overstayed his visa. He now qualified for the Green Card.

Prior to the granting of amnesty, his "friend" Kofi had reported him to Immigration as living illegally in the country. They did check his number in the telephone book but it wasn't listed.

Kofi could appreciate the Afolabi he once knew, but this new Afolabi he both hated and envied. He hated his good character because he saw it as a rebuke to his own and he was jealous of his knowledge. That also, was a rebuke to his indolence. He would have liked nothing better than to see him in trouble. This is what motivated him to report him to Immigration.

Unfortunately for both the Immigration officers and Kofi Randy, they didn't know how to get to him.

All the various alien groups organized parties, including, of course, the Africans. At their party, fortunately for Afolabi, the organizers included Joe Galas and other friends. Joe had posed bail for a great many African aliens. Since his marriage had nearly failed, he had turned his attention towards home - Africa. Therefore, as a token of thanks for the help he had given his brothers and sisters he was to chair the occasion. The planners refused to invite any government officials from Africa because of their indifference to the plight of arrested aliens.

It was surprising the way Joe had changed. Not only had he been able to employ a lot of his African brothers and sisters, but he and Kudjo Obalewa had opened the largest poultry farm in West Africa. They had employed a lot of secondary school graduates on the farms. This action had been applauded by many government officials. They praised them for their efforts to alleviate the hunger and job problem on the African continent.

Afolabi went to Times Square and had this poem printed on his T-shirt:

"Sing this song with me.

No more, no more.....

No more, no more.....

No more illegal alien.

No more, no more.

No more sweat shop.

No more, no more......

No more unable to go to Africa

No more, no more."

He wore his T-shirt to the party.

The music that night was superb. Even if you didn't want to dance to it, you couldn't help but sway with it. Afolabi, however, didn't have any partner. The women were either bluffing or just not available for strangers.

Sitting at a table in a corner was a tall, beautiful woman, her only partner a young boy about 11 years old. They seemed to be very unhappy. The boy was playing with a computer toy. Afolabi had an inkling that the woman might be Beatrice and the boy his son. But an African man with a dashiki kept getting up and dancing and returning to their table. The light was very dim, so he couldn't make out the two people clearly.

A BURNING DESIRE

All of a sudden he gathered courage and approached the woman and child as the man left again to dance.

"Excuse me," said Afolabi to the woman. Are you--" He was interrupted immediately as she answered his question with her own name.

"Beatrice? AFOLABI!" Beatrice leaped from her seat and hugged him tearfully. She then introduced him to the son that bore his name.

"Afolabi, this is your father!" she exclaimed. "Oh, Afolabi. I missed you so much," she said.

"All my life I've longed to know you," said little Afolabi, as he hugged his father affectionately. "Oh, if this is how the dead rise there would be no mourning," said his father.

"I've been looking for you all the time. When did you arrive in New York? Look at your son. I've been caring for him alone until now."

"I've been in New York a number of years already. Well, you certainly did a good job with Little Afolabi."

"Are you here by yourself? Are you married?" she questioned.

"Yes to the first question, no to the second. What about you?"

"No, I'm alone."

"Beautiful Beatrice, I'll marry you tomorrow. Oh, my African mother, you never let me down. I'll never let you down, either." We finally met each other."

"Son, this is your father, your only father except God in heaven. I'm too happy. Just too happy."

"Come on and let me introduce you to some friends," said Afolabi, leading them to the chairman's table.

A BURNING DESIRE

"Joe Galas, this is my wife, Beatrice. Kudjo Obalewa, this is Beatrice, the woman I spoke to you about in Africa, and this is our child, Afolabi," he said, proudly introducing his new-found family.

"You came here and you didn't bother to come up to us at the beginning of the party? Only when you--"

"I was very busy looking for them" Afolabi quickly explained. We have been separated these many years and just found each other again tonight! I hope all my dreams are going to come true. They are coming true, what with amnesty and--"

"Nice meeting you all," Beatrice interrupted, anxious to call it a night there and begin a beautiful night elsewhere.

"Please remember I also played a part in making your reunion possible, so don't write me off!" said Joe.

"Ditto," said Kudjo.

"Are you happy now?" Joe asked.

"Very happy," answered Afolabi and Beatrice simultaneously.

"Do you want a special song of reunion?"

"Not now. But thanks anyway. We're just rushing home together to celebrate our reunion after the long years of separation."

"Huh, what a celebration that's gonna be," said Kudjo with live and rich laughter, reminiscent of those laughters in Africa long ago.

Eyes followed them as they left. The 'brother' in the dashiki was upset because he had been trying to woo Beatrice all night without success. All well done and consumated, Afolabi hailed a taxi; and placing his two

A BURNING DESIRE

newly-found lovers in the back seat, he sat comfortably between them with his right leg placed over his left leg, while directing the driver of the taxi towards his house to begin a new life.

THE END

By CHIEF MORGAN ADZEI

A BURNING DESIRE - Part I

Chief Morgan Adzei. An historical novel that enveloped an African Orphan in his native African village and New York. The story described how formidable and heart-breaking obstacles were met by this daring and intelligent young man, while growing up in Africa. Arriving in New York City full of hopes and dreams at the turn of the century only to be destroyed by human weaknesses in present day society which consequently landed him hopelessly into an ocean of ignorance, suffering and self-hatred. However, with the help of his mother's apparition, Chief Adzei's protagonist was fished out alive and directed towards some great African-American Thinkers in Harlem where his African mind was liberated. Turning his mind to Africa ultimately, he turned the many woes of the African continent into wealth by giving directions and purpose to millions of his confused people and terminating the global exodus that hitherto engulfed the entire continent of Africa. Chief Adzei made his brothers and sisters find jobs from their own AFRICAN MINDS through this powerful novel: A BURNING DESIRE.

ISBN 0-910437-01-7   Price: $6.00 Paper

DEALERS & FUNDRAISERS: BULK RATES AVAILABLE FOR CHURCHES
                       AND RELIEF ORGANIZATIONS